D0941598

Paper Trail

Also by Barbara Snow Gilbert

Stone Water
Broken Chords

Paper Trail

Barbara Snow Gilbert

FRONT STREET
Asheville, North Carolina
2000

Acknowledgments

Several of the sources quoted in the documentary portions of this book are recommended for further reading on the subject. These materials include *False Patriots*, a comprehensive report on the roots of paramilitary antigovernment activity, and any other publications of the Southern Poverty Law Center. The SPLC is a private, nonprofit organization that includes the Militia Task Force, formed in 1994 to monitor developments in the antigovernment Patriot movement, and the Klanwatch Project, formed in 1979 to monitor white supremacist activity and to maintain current information on the status of hate groups. *Gathering Storm: America's Militia Threat*, by Morris Dees (chief trial counsel for the SPLC) with James Corcoran, reports a behind-the-scenes history of the movement and contains a more complete list of sources. The *Oklahoma Gazette* is a weekly news, politics, and arts newspaper that has provided in-depth coverage of the movement's activities and leaders within the state.

The author gratefully acknowledges and thanks the authors and publishers of these and of all news and research materials cited in the documentary portions of this book, for making their findings, observations, and expert opinions available for further study and commentary. All previously published reference materials are fully attributed in the text.

Library of Congress Cataloging-in-Publication Data
Paper trail / Barbara Snow Gilbert.
p. cm.
Summary: In hiding from the Soldiers of God, the Oklahoma antigovernment militia group whose members have now turned against him and his parents, a fifteen-year-old boy remembers what it was like to grow up among them.
ISBN 1-886910-44-8 (alk. paper)
[1. Militia movements—Fiction. 2. Right-wing extremists—Fiction. 3. Government, Resistance to—Fiction. 4. Oklahoma—Fiction.] I. Title.
PZ7.G3725 Pap 2000
[Fic]—dc21   00-024231

*To my sister Margaret, with thanks
for her help with each of my books*

Paper Trail

Voices in the Woods

The fifteen-year-old boy crawled on his elbows, wedging himself tight inside the fallen hollow tree. His jeans were some protection but his flannel shirt was not, and as he inched forward, the wood scraped his belly.

His goal was a window of light, a knothole, several inches ahead. The boy pushed the deep pocket of air out of his chest and collapsed his ribcage so that he breathed from only the top of his lungs. To narrow himself, he stretched his right arm up the crumbling insides of the log, then pulled his body after it. If he could make it to the knothole he would be able to see and breathe and, he was pretty sure, his boots would be far enough in to be hidden.

Someone was calling his name.

The boy stopped wriggling.

His mother. No. She was supposed to be running in the other direction, decoying the Soldiers of God away from him. The boy's father was the one who was supposed to circle back, and he wouldn't do so unless the woods were clear.

The boy edged up to the knothole. He blinked

against the light. And the distinctive crack of a Sako TRG-21 sniper rifle shattered the glassy stillness of the April morning.

He squeezed both eyes shut and sucked up a mouthful of grit as a second gunshot cracked the air. Or was the second shot only an echo? The boy was familiar with the games sound could play as it ricocheted off trees. He squeezed his eyes tighter.

Dry, papery, trashy sounds came next, like someone wadding notebook paper up close to his ear. But the sounds weren't paper, the boy knew. The same sorts of sounds had come from under the boy's and his mother's and his father's feet when the three of them had been running away only moments ago. The sounds were the leaves, dead and drifting since autumn, breaking as something fell.

Silence. Worse than the sounds.

He should look. Surely, the boy thought, that was why God had placed the knothole just so. Was why, maybe twenty years ago, when the log was still a living giant in these eastern Oklahoma backwoods, a branch at the very spot where the boy's eye was now had rotted and fallen off, unplugging the hole. Was why, years later, a storm blew in and toppled the tree at just the right angle. All of it so that the boy, at this moment, could see. Could see that in spite of the crack of the rifle, in spite of the breaking leaves and the silence after, his mother was all right. Sometimes even Soldiers of God missed.

Quick, he told himself. Before they came chasing

after their bullet. Quick, before they found the boy, eyes closed and twitching behind the knothole. The boy released the gritty gulp of air and opened his eyes. Bits of crushed leaves stuck to her face.

"Mom, Mom."

Now the day is over, night is drawing nigh.

"Remember the prayer at tuck-in time, Mom? Let me pray it for you now. For both of us."

Shadows of the evening steal across the sky.

"You cross-stitched the words on the hem of my pillowcase."

Lord, give the weary calm and sweet repose.

A thread of spit hung from her lip.

And with Thy tenderest blessing, may our eyelids close.

"Please, Mom, wipe it off. Mothers don't go around with threads of spit hanging like cobwebs. Wipe it off wipe it off WIPE IT OFF."

But already a fat red ant was climbing the strand.

The wound must be on the side away from the boy because he saw no blood or bullet hole. But he could see the angle of her head on her neck, and his chest began to rise and fall, pressing against the ragged insides of the log. Now he could barely whisper. "Oh."

Snap. Like a mousetrap, but there were no mousetraps in the forest. Probably a high-topped army boot, stepping on a branch, coming for a boy in a log.

"It's okay, Mom." The boy said his goodbyes softly between heaves. "Mom, don't worry. I'll be fine." To no one in particular he added, "I knew anyway. Ever since that ant started up."

Voices approached, calling one-word orders too muffled to make out. The leaves crunched close by, and hot urine flooded the inseams of the boy's Wrangler's. If the soldiers were alert, they could sniff their way to him.

They would defer to their best marksman, though they would no longer need a marksman. Taliferro, probably. Sean Taliferro could deliver shots in a half-inch cluster at one hundred yards.

Whoever the gunman was, he would slowly, calmly, maybe all the while shaking his head with regret over the orders, put the barrel of his rifle to the knot-hole. Or poke it up the end of the log, up between the boy's legs. Would the boy rather die from a bullet to his eye or from a bullet ripping vertically through him, organ by organ?

Or the soldiers might not end it so easily. They might keep their catch alive for their commander in chief, the Reverend General, the Fisher of Men himself.

Branches snapped and dust billowed as pair after pair of high-topped army boots exploded into the clearing. The boy barely breathed. His heart pumped fast and loud.

One set of trousers tramped up to the log, then stopped. The red and black patch stitched high on the outside right boot completely filled the boy's tiny window of vision—two M-16's, crisscrossed over the Christian sign of the fish.

The boy knew the emblem well. His parents paraded it openly. On a flag thumbtacked to the fake wood paneling in their Airway Deluxe mobile home. On a license plate wired to the bumper of their pickup. The fish and guns were even tattooed in fine-line indigo on his father's forearm.

The patch moved away, clearing the boy's view of another set of boots straddling his mother's body. The owner of the boots knelt and spoke. "Pupils fixed and dilated." Fingerless black knit gloves gently examined her head, then pressed the vein behind her ear. The gloves lifted her torso off the leaves, exposing the nape of her neck and one soft curl at the hairline.

A few yards away, someone began to vomit. The inspecting soldier ignored the throwing up and continued to report. "Entry, back of skull, upper left quadrant. Exit, right temple."

The gloves laid her down and her head wobbled back. The gold dove wedding ring that she wore on a necklace under her blouse slipped into the niche at the base of her throat.

A third set of boots paced. "Lord," the soldier murmured over and over as he walked back and forth, "but this is sorrowful duty."

"Sorrowful waste of good looks, too," another soldier answered.

The boy strained to recognize the voices but didn't. Maybe the log muffled the pitch. Or maybe these were new guys. There were always new guys.

"Bag the body," the officer in charge ordered. "And remove it to base camp."

The commanding officer was right, the boy

thought. The object on the other side of the knothole was "it," not his mother. The boy's mother was a beauty who sat for hours dangling a bare foot, memorizing poems. The boy's mother was an artist when she held a needle in her hand, her fingertips hard and shiny because she never used a thimble. The boy's mother was a dreamer who used to scoop a little boy up in her swirling yellow flowered skirt, swaying with him on the porch swing as she read him fairy tales.

You must not think of her.

The voice in his head was right. The boy closed his eyes and tried to empty his mind. Slowly he opened his lids again.

A soldier unzipped a vinyl bag and rolled the body onto it. The commander strode back and forth giving orders. "Designate this site Alpha. And get me a sitrep on the two additional targets."

Static erupted, then was tuned away. A second voice spoke distinctly, as if into the radio, stating identification and position and relaying orders.

"We'll hold Alpha," the officer continued, the second voice repeating him into the radio. "It looked like she was coming to this spot. Maybe the clearing's a rendezvous point. The other targets may rejoin Alpha if they are still up and moving."

The boy flinched. The other targets were him and his father; of course they were still up and moving. But then he remembered the echo. Or second gunshot. A second bullet could have found another victim. His father could be lying in his own heap, out of view and earshot, waiting to be bagged by a different squad of soldiers.

The boy began to pant. His chest heaved faster and faster and the tree's insides crumbled around him. Would God let a fifteen-year-old boy lose both parents in one day?

No.

He closed his eyes and conjured his father. David Morgan would know that his wife had circled back. Even now he must be watching, biding his time.

The boy's breathing slowed. The image of his father sharpened, perched on a limb, hidden behind the new spring foliage, his silver dove flashing in the sunlight. The boy's mother kept her ring hidden, which suited her. Maybe because she kept lots of things hidden, like the bottle of brandy in the cupboard, behind the dangling teacups—

Put your mother away. Find an empty cell back in the honeycomb of your brain and pour her into it. You can look for that sweet cell eventually, but not for a long time. Not until you are completely out of this.

The boy went back to his father. It was bold, the way he wore the silver dove. Other Soldiers of God owned jewelry. Old Davis Johns wore a diamond pinkie ring. Jim Redhawk kept a coin from Desert Storm on a chain around his neck. But diamonds and chunky links had nothing in common with a delicate silver dove—

Something covered the knothole. The boy's fresh air was cut off!

His eyes popped open but now there was nothing to see. There was a scent, though. Rubber. Whatever was covering the knothole smelled of rubber. A boot sole. One of the soldiers had propped his boot over the knothole. But a stiff boot sole couldn't completely seal a knothole, he didn't think.

The boy located a thin ribbon of air and concentrated on sucking it into his mouth. He willed his heartbeat slower.

He was going to get through this. He was.

The boy returned to his conjuring. He saw the way his father's gray eyes glowed, dilated from fixing themselves, too long, on the boy's hiding place. He imagined how, mane of silver hair flying, his father would pounce like a wild animal to rescue him if the soldier with his boot propped jumped back, warned by a breath or a sniffle from inside the log. If his father was out there. And he was, the boy was sure. Unless he was already dead, or—

The boy stopped breathing.

Or not coming back. Not coming back because he had been called to Washington.

Abandoning his wife and son for Washington? The boy's father might be capable of that, the boy thought, as he blacked out.

Scraps

Patriots come from all regions of the country and all walks of life.... They include tax protesters, millennialists, survivalists, Populists, freemen, constitutionalists, neo-Nazis, Skinheads, Klansmen, Identity believers, Christian Reconstructionists, secessionists, militant abortion foes, radical anti-environmentalists, and gun enthusiasts.

— from "United by Hate: Patriots Share Rage Against Government," *False Patriots*, p. 6*

The most highly organized of the Patriot groups are the militias, paramilitary forces operating in hundreds of small, relatively disconnected, units nationwide.

— from "A Diversity of Rebels: The Patriot Movement Crosses Old Ideological Boundaries," *False Patriots*, p. 14

Of the 435 Patriot groups identified by the Intelligence Project, 171 were militias.... In its count, the Intelligence Project found Patriot groups operating in every state in the nation.

— from "The World of 'Patriots,'" SPLC's *Intelligence Report*, Spring 1999 (issue 94), p. 11

*Southern Poverty Law Center, *False Patriots: The Threat of Antigovernment Extremists* (Montgomery, Alabama: SPLC, 1996).

With about five million followers, [the Patriot movement] is a movement that exists at the fringe of American life and politics....

There is, however, one thing [all those in the movement] hold in common: a relentless loathing and a deep hatred for the federal government.

— from *Gathering Storm*, p. 30*

*Morris Dees with James Corcoran, *Gathering Storm: America's Militia Threat* (New York: HarperCollins, 1996).

I remember spinning on the barstool.

One. Two. I tucked my legs and pushed off, spotting the "Miller Time" clock to keep from getting too dizzy. Three. Four.

We had just moved to Red Cedar, so I was five, way too little to be legal at the bar of Roy Roye's Game Room and Lounge. But Roy Roye didn't seem to care and I guess nobody else did either.

The room was full when Jim Redhawk, who my dad had just challenged to a darts match, spoke up in too loud a voice. "What *are* you, Morgan, wearin' a ring like that, some kinda peacenik?"

I was only up to twenty spins but the lounge got quiet and I stopped.

Roy Roye put down the ashtray he was wiping. The old man on the next stool with his Bible open on the counter looked up from the red-lettered pages.

I was still a little dizzy when Ronald Murry dropped his foosball handles and turned to my father. "Yeah, Morgan." He grinned. "Me and my brother Johnny"—he nodded at his twin on the opposite side

of the table—"us two always suspected you got pacifist leanings."

It scared me, the way the Murry brothers laughed.
But my dad just picked up the next dart.

"I think you boys might need to read the Good
Book more often," my father said calmly, but loud
enough that everyone could hear. "You've gotten your
testaments a bit confused. Ask the gentleman with the
Bible over there. It's Noah's *Old* Testament bird—coming back with that olive branch in his beak—that's the
peacemaker."

My father narrowed one eye at the target and
cocked his elbow. "My bird—" The fresh tattoo on his
forearm rocked back and forth as he set the motion.
"—is a *New* Testament dove. Entirely different species."

He released the dart and it needle-nosed into the
bull's-eye. Then he faced the Murry brothers and
spoke as if he were swearing allegiance. "My dove is
the sign of the Holy Spirit, signifying my ordainment
to the just and righteous cause of God's earthly militia."

I tipped my head to the side and looked at him. The
silver band was his *wedding* ring, and my mother had
a gold one just like it.

She had told me the story of the two little doves a
thousand times. About how, when they met, they
bowed and cooed and smoothed each other's feathers.
About the way the daddy fed the mommy seeds on
their wedding day, and built a nest of grass and twigs.
About how they fed their babies pigeon's milk out of

their throats. And especially about the way the two doves would always stay together, as long as they were both alive.

I started to say something. "But Daddy—"

My father cut me off. "You tell 'em, sir," he said to the gentleman sitting beside me. He dropped the remaining darts into Jim Redhawk's palm, walked over, and tapped the pages of the old man's Bible. "Because it sounds to me like some of the people in this room need a little scripture lesson."

Then he picked me off the barstool and carried me out of there sideways under his arm.

How Time Got Unplugged

Cold. Inside the log, the boy shivered himself awake. The rubbery smell was gone. How long had he been unconscious, in a coma, asleep, whatever it was that he had been?

It would be the easiest thing, the boy thought as he began to stir, to just not return—to consciousness, or Red Cedar, or the nightmare of the Soldiers of God. Stay in the log and go back to sleep and forget it all. Except that he was freezing.

He opened his eyes. But had he really? Open or closed there was no difference, everything was just as black. He closed his lids and opened them again, testing.

This was utter dark. No flashlights. No porch lights. No light from the Luceros' TV turned backwards in the picture window next door so Jake and Ricardo could watch wrestling from their lawn chairs. This was the dark of a cold spring night, alone, in the forest.

Not alone.

The boy held still and listened, but the voice in his

head was quiet.

He listened harder, for boots, or orders, or crunching leaves. He heard nothing, though he knew those sounds would be back soon enough.

He tried to wiggle his toes, but he was numb from the knees down. His feet were the most exposed part of him, and the lack of feeling there scared him. All sorts of nocturnal animals could be lurking around the log, returning to their stolen den. The boy's left leg was half an inch shorter than his right, had been since birth, though no one had noticed until he started to walk, when the barely perceptible hitch in his step showed up. Maybe raccoons were nibbling his long side right now, he thought, evening him up, and he just couldn't feel it.

Your cowboy boots are sharkskin. Nibbling won't hurt you.

Well, raccoons or not, he had to get out. He remembered what his father had told him as the three of them ran through the forest, fleeing for their lives.

"You're a target," his dad had said. "We all are."

Confused, the boy had looked back and forth between his parents, panting as they ran. His family, targets? Of the Soldiers of God? Why?

It was at that moment they found themselves in a clearing. Dropping to one knee, the boy's father crouched behind a giant fallen log. He motioned his gasping son and wife down with him. Still breathing hard, his father put his hand on his son's shoulder. "I am a federal agent. Undercover FBI."

Open-mouthed, the boy could only stare at his father and clutch the stitch in his side. By the time what his father was telling him began to sink in, his parents were already stuffing him up his hiding place, covering his boots with leaves at the open end.

And then his father's voice came again, through the knothole this time, over the boy's head. "I will circle back when it's clear, make sure they're off your trail, and then I'm going to the diner. I can file my report from there. I have to do it, I have critical information that could save lives. But I will come back for you the first minute I can. If I don't ... if something happens ... the diner is safe. Meet there."

The boy's mother pressed a kiss through the knothole—he heard her lips and saw her callused fingertips—and then his parents were gone.

Now, inside the log, tears slipped down the boy's cheeks.

Crying will only make it harder to breathe. It is hard enough already.

The boy stopped crying. Working up from his toes, he flexed his muscles. He had located everything except his right arm when he remembered reaching up the log to squeeze the final inches to the knothole. His right arm must still be up there. What if the log were open at that end, too? His stirrings might only have sent the coons to the other entrance to snack on his numb fingers. If only he could bring his right arm back down. IF ONLY HE COULD BRING HIS RIGHT ARM BACK DOWN!

Hush, now. Thoughts like that could make a boy crazy.

The boy reached with his toes back toward the opening through which he had come, and rippled his body down the matching inch.

He was wet and panting. Wood chips were falling into his eyes, burning. But none of it mattered. Because in that one inch the possibility of getting out of the log had caught him. If his hunters were outside, waiting in the dark with their night-scopes aimed, it didn't matter. Anything was better than staying in this claustrophobic, airless place.

He could breathe deep and expand his ribs and burst the log open from the inside. No, that wasn't real. But the feeling was. He couldn't, he couldn't, he couldn't stand it in here another second—

Don't think of seconds. Unplug time.

It was good advice. Because at this glacial rate of one inch per try, he would have to stand many more seconds and minutes and possibly even hours.

If he could even get out. Had his right arm come the inch with him? His right arm might keep him stuck up this dead tree forever, to truly become food for coons. He had to get out of the log. Now.

No. Not now.

Okay, not now. Time was unplugged. He would get out when he would get out.

Better.

The boy reached his toes back another inch.

I remember standing on the seat of my chair, trying to match the words we were singing to the words my father was tracking for me in the hymnal. I must have been about six or seven because I could read, just not as fast as my dad's finger was moving.

My father sang the melody in firm tones.

"And the voice I hear, falling on my ear..."

My mom stood on the other side of me with her arm wrapped around my legs. She sang too, but faintly, like always.

The seats were folding ones, and Davis Johns, the older gentleman in the row behind us, rested his open Bible on the back of my chair and held it steady. My dad thanked him with a nod and kept singing.

By the second verse I was ignoring my father's finger and singing the chorus from memory.

"He walks with me, and He talks with me ..."

Around me, people began to sway—except for my mother, who never did. With my cowboy boots planted in the seat, I leaned from side to side and searched the mix of T-shirts and camouflage for Tony Rossetti, my new friend from Sunday school. Tony didn't usually come to Soldiers of God services, but today his grandfather, Jim Redhawk, had brought him along.

I located Jim Redhawk on the aisle with his hands folded in front of him. Except when he played darts his hands shook, and he always kept them like that. There was a space between Jim Redhawk and my Sunday school teacher, Cherry Martindale. Probably Tony was slouched in the gap, punching his Game Boy.

Ronald and Johnny Murry, the song leaders, called out, "Last chorus," and my eyes went back to my father's finger tracking along the page. I swayed farther left and right and sang louder with my dad.

"...His voice to me is calling. And He walks with me, and He talks with me, and He tells me I am his own; And the joy we share as we tarry there, none other has ever known."

Everyone clapped and my parents each held a hand as I hopped to the floor. There was scooting and shuffling as people sat down. Now I was hidden again.

Speaking began at the front of the room and I tugged my mom's yellow flowered skirt. She bent down; I wrapped my finger around a blond lock and pulled her face to mine. She rinsed her hair in rainwater and honeysuckle oil, and she smelled like our garden.

"Can I color?" I whispered.

She kissed me on the cheek. "Yes."

I crawled off the seat and slid the coloring book and

crayons I had been given in Sunday school out from under my chair. Kneeling on the creaking floorboards, facing backwards and using my seat as a desk, I bent over the work.

By the time the Murry brothers announced the final hymn, my knees were sore and my palms were waxy. I wrote "To Mom" over the words "We do God's work" printed at the bottom of the page. The song started and I passed the book to her and climbed up on my chair.

"Onward Christian soldiers, marching as to war..."

Beside me, my mother stayed seated, head down, staring at my picture on her lap. Maybe I had colored outside of the lines too much. I leaned back to see.

A Soldier of God looked out from the page. With one hand he lifted a baby bird back to its nest. With the other he gripped an M-16.

The gun was accurate, I knew from Sunday school, and the camo colors were right. I had gone a little out of the lines, though.

My father reached over and nudged my mother. She looked up, then turned the picture a fraction toward him. My dad kept singing but he skipped a few words, even though both of us knew this one by heart.

I swung my arms and marched in place and Davis Johns held my chair. "Like a mighty army moves the Church of God," my dad and I belted out.

My mother closed the coloring book and stood up, but she never sang a word of that song.

Scraps

"Jesus Christ Was Not A Pacifist."

> — from the field manual of the Militia of Montana, quoted in "Justifying the Guns," *False Patriots*, p. 12

[T]his area has become a magnet for many in the radical right, men and women who are drawn to a place where the land is still cheap, the living is private and the population is white.... [The region is] peopled with "pretty well-armed" Christians.

> — from "Hills of Rebellion," SPLC's *Intelligence Report*, Summer 1999 (issue 95), pp. 31-33, quoting Nord Davis, Jr., organizer of Northpoint Tactical Teams

And then there is the militant Jesus Christ, said [Pastor Pete] Peters, who urged his apostles to arm themselves with swords, even if they had to sell their garments to do so. The sword in Jesus' day was equivalent to an M16 in our day, he said, and it is the duty of all Christians "not only to own one, but be able to use one."

> — from *Gathering Storm*, p. 21

A Fixed Point

Out of the log at last, the boy crept behind a tree. Probably he didn't need to stay hidden. If the Soldiers of God knew where he was—if they'd been watching as his body slithered free of the log like a snake from its skin—they'd have executed him long ago.

The boy rose stiffly, ignoring the pain in his shoulder. It felt great to be standing. Afraid spitting would make too much noise, he raked the bitter bits from his teeth and dribbled his saliva to the ground. He wiped his nose on his shirttail and picked the crust out of his eyes. Puffing on his numb fingers, he managed to button the cuffs of his flannel shirt, then curled his hands inside the sleeves and wrapped his arms around his chest.

The Soldiers of God were big on wilderness training. The boy owned several survival manuals and he knew the techniques. He had to *do* something, occupy his mind, stay busy.

Okay, okay. He stamped the ground. He was doing something. His right shoulder might be dislocated from being stuck up that log. His old injury in that arm, his passing arm, was hurting him, but he was breathing and thinking and stamping the ground. The next thing he had to do was to figure out where he was, so that he didn't end up running *toward* the Soldiers of God base camp instead of away.

The boy closed his eyes and pictured a map of LeFlore County. There was Red Cedar, the little dot where federal highway 59 turned into 259 and crossed state highway 63. North lay the Ouachita National Forest. South was Octavia, then Smithville, then the McCurtain County Wilderness. Arkansas and more national forest were east, and the Kiamichi Mountains were west. Now all he had to do was put himself in the back of the pickup on the thin line of highway on the map driving south, and replay the tape.

He didn't want to do it.

I will walk you through it.

The boy breathed deep, exhaled slowly, and closed his eyes.

It was Saturday morning and they—he and his mom, Blanche, and his dad, David, and his dog, Pet— were in his father's truck. They were going to the annual spring war games at the Soldiers of God base camp, heading south out of Red Cedar on 259.

Do you remember making the turn onto the gravel road? The turn's twelve miles from town.

The film had started running behind the boy's eyes.

They passed the one-pump Git 'N Go with the twisting barber's pole on the porch. The high school, deserted because it was a Saturday. Dead Man's Curve.

The rising elevation of the highway. There it was, the unmarked road to the base camp, and yes, they had exited. He remembered the gravel clinking against the underside of the truck.

How far did you go on the gravel turnoff?

As they drove down the road, the boy leaned against the truck cab to block the wind. That was when, facing backwards, he saw the militia's Dodge minivan with tinted black glass behind them, closing fast.

He looked back into the cab. His father's eyes were fixed on the rear-view mirror. His mother was studying her own outside mirror. The first tiny shard of concern forced its way into the boy's brain.

Which way were you heading at that point?

The road followed the curve of the land, so it varied, but basically they were headed east, into the hills.

So the truck was going east when you jumped out?

That was skipping ahead a little. He was going to have to go through it to be sure.

The boy gathered Pet, who up until then had been sliding around on her nails, into his arms. He looked back at his parents, their eyes still fixed on the mirrors, and that was when he saw the station wagon parked sideways across the road ahead of them on the first hairpin turn. He knew the car, with the body stripped down to the primer and a fish and guns spray-painted on the side. His parents must have seen it too, because their heads moved forward a notch and his father took his foot off the gas.

The soldiers posted in front of the station wagon

placed one leg forward and raised their weapons to shoulder-fire position. Old Sal, the militia's Doberman, stood alert on her chain.

The boy's father rapped his knuckles on the glass and shouted, twirling his finger in the air. They were going to turn around and try to get back to the highway to make a break. He motioned his son to get down and hold on.

Make a break from exactly who or what, the boy wondered, but he kept his arms around Pet and braced himself low in the corner. The moment he was set, the truck skidded and spun.

The force tore Pet from his arms. Some wooden crates that were roped into the back of the truck slammed against the steel sides and tipped. Books scattered. Tires spun. The truck bed pitched sharply and his mother's rosewood china chest slid out from under a tarp.

The boy stared at the china chest and the rest of the things that had spilled, his mother's poetry books and his father's militia research. His father collected publications about the Patriot movement, providing the Soldiers of God with better information about the state of their own movement nationwide than they could ever have obtained on their own. But what were the books and articles doing here? And the boy's own football? And the family Bible? That's when it hit him: his family had been packed to *leave*.

The boy's father was already out of the truck cab, yelling at the boy and his mother to run. The boy leaped and, doors still swinging, the boy and his mother and father plunged into the woods.

Pet was barking. The boy looked back to see just the top of her head in the truck. She must be hurt because usually she vaulted easily from the bed.

The boy stopped behind a tree. By now the soldiers could have the pickup in their sights. If the boy called Pet to join him, they might open fire on the sudden movement, mistaking her for one of them. But he couldn't just leave his dog.

He called and Pet jumped—to a burst of automatic fire. And then she lay flat on the ground.

The boy waited for his dog to lift her head and look up at him, but she didn't. He went back to running away with his parents, wiping his eyes to keep the ground from wavering.

He should have skipped that last part, about Pet.

Take some time. Don't start again until you're ready.

The boy took a shuddery breath, then thought back. They hadn't made the first hairpin, so they were still headed east when the truck spun off the road. Facing west now, he and his mom and his dad jumped out and ran to the right. That put the three of them running north, into the woods.

How far did you run?

His mom was ahead, and then his dad, and then him, because he had taken that extra time to call his dog. His dad was frantically motioning for him to catch up. The boy managed to, but it was hard, because he had a terrible stitch in his side. It seemed like hours, running with that stitch.

People can't run for hours with a stitch. How far, really?
The boy could run a 10k in forty-eight minutes.
Even with one leg off by half an inch?
His leg wasn't a big deal. It didn't hold him up. But a 10k in forty-eight was about his limit, and when his family found the clearing with the log, he was way past his limit, though not because of the distance. He'd been running dead-out in the woods with a stitch, and hiding was his best chance because he couldn't go any farther. He thought, altogether, it was a lot less than 10k. Maybe half. About three miles.

That's it. You did it. You got this little patch of earth down to the size of a postage stamp.
The boy leaned back against a tree, let out a deep breath, and imagined his route to this point on the map.

You're three miles north of the gravel turnoff, a little way east of 259.
That meant, if he faced north, the highway was on his left and Red Cedar was nine miles ahead. All he had to do was find north.

The boy remembered reading in one of his survival books about making a compass with a needle and a silk scarf and a bowl of water. He shook his head. Like a person stranded in the wilderness would have a needle and a silk scarf and a bowl of water! No, he needed the stars. He looked up, but the trees blocked the sky. If he just started walking, hoping for a clearing, he'd lose himself all over because he'd have no idea which way he was heading. And after all that work to find where he was, too. He looked up again. Maybe that was the solution.

Perched high in a southern yellow pine, the boy scanned the night sky.

Take the two stars at the front of the Big Dipper. Draw a line. There, the North Star. The diner was about nine miles ahead, in the direction of the star, up 259. It might even be possible to see the snaking highway from here, although he wouldn't know until the sun came up.

Which was okay. Because he felt suddenly exhausted, but safe, and fixed, at least, in this tree with his eyes on the wonderful, wonderful North Star.

The boy turned up his collar. He straddled the branch and unbuckled his tooled leather belt. He fastened the leather around the tree trunk, then looped his good left arm through the strap as a guard against falling. Resting his cheek against the bark, he breathed in the pine scent and watched the sky to the east. He could have been almost comfortable if it hadn't been for…things he wasn't thinking about.

At least he wasn't down there on the ground anymore, a trapped animal crouching in the dark. And he wasn't lost in the night, looking for bearings he couldn't possibly find until morning, using up calories and strength. He knew exactly where he was. He was fixed at this spot at the top of this southern yellow pine, and he was keeping his eye on dead north.

Scraps

The incident occurred on a public road outside the organization's heavily guarded 20-acre compound.... [T]he guards "chased [plaintiff and her 19-year-old son] for over two miles, shot at them with assault rifles, detained them, battered them and threatened to kill them."

> — from Patrick McMahon, "Assault, Terror Cited in Suit Against Aryan Nations," *USA Today*, Feb. 15, 1999, p. 4A, quoting lawsuit allegations

The most sophisticated training camps have 700-yard sniping ranges and demolition grounds for bomb testing. Target practice takes place with automatic weapons, large caliber machine guns and .50-caliber sniper rifles.

> — from "Paramilitary Training: Militias Prepare for Confrontation with Government," *False Patriots*, p. 20

Patriot terrorists have access to some of the most lethal weapons available—including powerful explosives, biochemical agents and sophisticated, military-style arms....

Among the weapons, explosives and other equipment stolen from military bases are Stinger missiles, LAW rockets, plastic explosives, night-vision goggles, automatic rifles and pistols, hand grenades, blasting caps and military-grade ammunition....

Recipes and blueprints for a variety of powerful explosives—including the formula for ANFO (the ammonium nitrate and fuel oil bomb that tore apart the federal building in Oklahoma City)—are readily available.

— from "The Tools of Terrorism," *False Patriots*, p. 25

"The [Patriot] movement has become more militant, and the death toll has increased. It's truly ready and willing to wage war against the government."

— Daniel Levitas, author and student of the radical right,
quoted in "'Patriot' Numbers Decrease, But Movement
Gets Meaner," *SPLC Report* (vol. 28, no. 2), June 1998, p. 3

I remember taking turns with Tony, licking honey off the knife. Third grade had let out for the summer at noon that day and the two of us sat cross-legged on my kitchen floor, backpacks strapped to our shoulders. We were waiting for my mom to finish the reading lesson she was giving Roy Roye.

I dipped the knife into the mostly empty Mason jar. My mom wouldn't care that we had used up the honey because Roy Roye brought a new jar every time he came. But my mother would want to know why we had used up a whole loaf of her homemade bread. Well, Tony and I were ready for her.

I handed the knife to Tony, who dipped and licked. We were going to ride our bikes a mile out of town to Bandit's Hollow, an outcropping of rock with a little cave. The only catch was, my mother had never allowed the two of us to go so far by ourselves.

We had carefully planned our strategy. Let my mom observe us making sandwiches. Clean up after ourselves and stay quiet while she tutored, proving our responsibility. But now, with Roy Roye struggling to sound out the little verse I could have recited in seconds, the strategy seemed like a bad one.

I held my breath as Roy finished the last line, afraid that on the other side of the cupboard that divided our kitchen from our living room, my mother might turn to another selection in her dog-eared book of poems.

My mom's head appeared over the cabinet. She didn't rest her arms; nobody was allowed to lean there for fear of jiggling the china tea set with the gold "LeF" monogram inside. I didn't know what the initials stood for, but I knew it must be something important, considering the gentle way she handled the dishes when she made herself tea. There was an empty rosewood chest meant to hold the entire set, but my mother always kept the pieces out—pitcher, creamer, sugar bowl, saucers, and cups dangling from hooks—where she could admire them through the plexiglass. There was another fragile thing in that cupboard too, but it was a thing we never talked about. Already, though, I had begun to keep track, and I knew how often a new bottle took its turn behind the teacups.

"Okay, boys." My mother looked down at us on the floor, a finger marking her place in the gilt-edged book. "What's up?"

Tony and I stood in unison. Carefully I placed the knife and empty jar in the sink. Then I opened my backpack under my mother's nose, revealing neat stacks of sandwiches wrapped in wax paper. We presented our case.

My mother thought for a minute, then consulted Roy Roye. "Do you think these boys are old enough for such an adventure?"

When she used the word "adventure" I knew it was a slam dunk. She and Roy went on discussing, but I was already tying my backpack and trading looks with Tony.

"Tony," she said, turning to us, "have you asked your mother?"

"No, but my mom wouldn't care." Tony's mother was young enough to be his sister. She never paid attention to anything he did.

My mother looked at Tony for a moment and then followed up. "And what would your Grandpa Redhawk say?"

Tony thought for a second. "He'd say okay."

My mom nodded. "And I say okay, too."

Tony and I were already halfway out the aluminum door.

"But with a few rules," my mom called, following Roy and the two of us outside.

Tony and I leaped off the porch and ran for our bikes. Roy waved goodbye and headed across the road.

My mom trailed after us, her finger still in her book. "Don't go to the quarry." The town swimming hole was an abandoned quarry pit. "I don't want you swimming unless I come with you."

"No swimming," we answered quickly.

She smiled. "And be home by dinnertime."

Neither of us owned a watch, but we knew "dinnertime" meant before the sun began to set.

Kickstand up, hands on the bars, I whistled for Pet, my half-grown puppy, who came running. My parents had picked the collie-Lab-mutt mix from Cherry Martindale's pack of strays for my ninth birthday.

"Look out for Pet and stay together."

"Okay, okay, okay," we chanted.

She kissed me on the cheek and I rolled my eyes. Then she kissed Tony, who, I noticed, didn't seem to mind. Issuing instructions, she strolled beside us, arms folded on her chest as we walked our bikes into the middle of the dirt road.

"Come home safe and sound and on time," she hollered after us as we pushed off, "and I'll know you are grown-up boys."

She was still standing in the middle of the road shading her eyes with her book when we pedaled around the corner.

We played bandits and marshals, trappers and traders, and Indians and army. Pet assumed roles as a black bear, army scout, and tribal dog, and we shared our sandwiches with her. From our lookout we spied on the big kids who passed by on their way to the swimming hole. And when we rode back down the trail late that afternoon, I actually felt older than when we had ridden up.

Where the asphalt began at the top of Hill Street, we stopped, Pet between us, and straddled our bikes. We surveyed the horizon. It would be thirty minutes before the edge of the sun touched the treetops, but Pet's tongue was lolling.

We would stop at the Git 'N Go at the bottom of the hill. The store had an outside water fountain and Pet could drink from our hands. Then we'd impress my mom by arriving home early.

I tipped my bike over the brink and coasted down, sitting a little to the left on my seat, the way I always did to make up for my short leg. Passing the Murry brothers' tidy house on the corner, I raised my arm at a right angle, signaling the upcoming turn. There was no one but Tony to see, but it was a reminder to both of us that the timing was critical. You had to slow down enough to turn sharply at the bottom or else risk a blind, sweeping arc into the highway. There was never much traffic on 63, but the turn was a little scary anyway.

My bike was an old one with foot brakes. As I began to slow down, pressing back lightly on the pedals, the long honk of trucker's horn sounded up the hill. Picturing a two-ton logging rig racing toward the intersection of Hill and Highway 63, I slammed on the brakes.

My back tire skidded out from under me and my bicycle began to tip. Fighting to stay upright, I gripped the handlebars and managed to aim the front wheel into the parking lot behind the Git 'N Go, but I could see that I was going to go down in glittering gravel and broken glass. The cement bumped hard as I hit. With my right side burning from my elbow to my shin, I slid to a stop.

I lay on my back, backpack smashed under me, with no air in my lungs. My right arm, which must have hit the ground first, throbbed.

Pet licked my face. As I began to breathe again, the wheel of Tony's bike rolled into view and the roar of a semi passed by on the highway.

Tony dropped his bicycle. I turned my head on the hot pavement to see him running toward the back door of the store.

Shelly Williams, who managed the Git 'N Go with her husband, Vince, was Red Cedar's unofficial medic. Except for maybe my mom, she was also the prettiest woman in town. She had dimples and a ponytail of curly red hair, and I was embarrassed at the thought of her finding me fallen. I sat up as she and Tony came jogging back.

"Where does it hurt the most?" she asked.

"My arm."

She made me move my fingers and examined my bones and joints. "I don't think anything is flat-out broken," she said. "But there could be a fracture or a chipped bone."

She helped me up. "I'll give you aspirin, but if the pain keeps up, you're gonna need an x-ray."

The two of them put their arms around my waist and walked me toward the store. We passed my bike, crashed against the trash dumpster with the front fender twisted and the seat off. A list of the things a nine-year-old boy with a fractured arm and a wrecked bike couldn't do for the rest of the summer began to run through my head.

Inside the store, I braced my arm against my body and climbed into the barber's chair where Vince Williams cut hair. Dogs weren't allowed in the Git 'N Go, but when Pet lay down at the foot of the chair, nobody said anything.

Shelly Williams took alcohol wipes, scissors, bandages, and tweezers from her first-aid kit and arranged the supplies on the counter. She hiked the chair as high as it would go and knelt in front of me, studying the bits of glass and gravel embedded in my knees.

She held the ripped flaps of denim out of the way. "There are easier ways to make cutoffs." She patted my leg and smiled.

I tried to smile back but couldn't manage.

She slid the phone within my reach. "I guess you better call your mama," she said, and my eyes began to fill.

"Here, darlin'." Quickly she picked a green apple tearjerker out of the jar on the counter and put it into my scraped-up hand.

My arm hurt when I peeled off the cellophane, but she was waiting so I did it anyway and put the candy in my mouth.

Shelly Williams turned to Tony. "Them green apple tearjerkers," she said, "they been known to make a grown man's eyes water." Then she put the phone in my lap and started to tweeze.

Acorns or Candy

The boy unhooked his arms from the belt strapped around the trunk of the pine tree. The sky had lightened and the stars were disappearing. Craning his neck away from the coming dawn, he searched for some sign of Highway 259.

About a mile off, there was a precise, man-made cut in the carpet of hardwoods and evergreens. If he went higher he could possibly see the ribbon of asphalt. He eyed the fragile branches above him. His shoulder still hurt from being extended so long inside the log, and his old fracture had throbbed steadily through the night. Any more climbing would be painful. Even more important, if he went higher, he would be above the foliage line.

He closed his eyes and listened, but he heard none of the usual sounds of war games—no jeeps bumping along creek beds, or revving motors, or rifles firing blanks—only a woodpecker drilling somewhere in the mist. The boy could see why his parents would choose a war games weekend to secretly leave town. After the Saturday morning assembly, the army would disperse in the field. Games were always a little chaotic, and no one would realize the boy's family was missing until the army reassembled at dusk on Sunday.

But the Soldiers of God must have discovered his father's identity and his plans to flee, and the games had become a ruse to get his family alone on the gravel road. Because hear them or not, the Soldiers of God were out there, the boy knew, and it wasn't any kind of a game. Right now they would be shedding their night goggles and saying their morning prayers. And, as of first light one moment ago, the boy was much more vulnerable.

The boy slipped his belt back into the loops of his jeans and reviewed what he had decided. It would be too dangerous to walk or hitch along Highway 259 because a good share of the passing vehicles would be militia. But he could use the highway as a guide. He would keep to the trees. All around him were virgin woods so he wouldn't have to cross any roads or barbed wire, although Turtle Creek might give him trouble. "Creek" was an accurate enough name for the waterway at the end of a dry summer, but in the spring Turtle Creek was more like Turtle River. Well, the boy was a good swimmer. The worst that would happen was that he would get wet. When he got to town he would circle and creep up to the diner from the gully behind. An apartment had been added on to the back of the building, and there was a private back door.

Feeling set, the boy dangled one foot, felt for the

first branch, shifted his weight, and began to climb down. When he reached the lowest branch, he dropped to the rug of brown needles.

His shoulder was searing. He took off his flannel shirt. The early morning air was cold, but he still had an undershirt and the chill was nothing compared to the pain. He folded the shirt into a triangle, knotted one sleeve to one shirttail, and looped the fabric over his neck, arranging the weight of his right arm in the sling.

Already he was walking, establishing a rhythm. To avoid circling, he wound between the trees, passing the first on the left, the second on the right, the third on the left. For the first time since this all began, the boy noticed he was hungry.

Acorns are nutritious.

Without breaking stride, he reached down with his good arm and scooped up a few. He knew from his books that the bitter nuts contained vitamins, but he had never actually tasted one before. He let the acorns sift back to the ground but held on to the last one and flipped off the cap.

Hunger and thirst weren't a serious problem. A person could go many days without food, several without water, and the boy had to hike only nine miles. But hunger and thirst were an annoyance.

The boy put the acorn into his mouth and sucked on it, ignoring the awful taste. He would pretend it was candy.

—

By the time the day had warmed, the boy had sucked four acorns to a soft pulp. He spit the remains of the last one out and squinted up at the sun, high in the sky. Running three miles the day before and hiking all morning in cowboy boots had rubbed a blister on his heel. It must be close to noon, but his distance, or lack of it, was a disappointment.

After creeping west until he could just make out 259, he had made the turn north. Twice he had stopped and hidden to see if anyone was following him, but he had seen no sign of the Soldiers of God. No more hiding. And no more passing trees on the left and right, now that he had the highway to guide him. He had figured on being to the diner by now, but at this rate he'd be lucky to make Red Cedar by dark.

The boy sat down and pulled off his boot and sock. With a stick he slit the blister's loose, pasty skin. Clear liquid trickled out. He packed leaves over the wound, pulled on his sock—rotated so that a clean spot covered the blister—and slid his heel back into the snug boot leather.

Ready to move again, he paused just long enough to run his hands through his hair. A bump. His fingers searched for more of the small, raised spots and found a half-dozen of the creatures, already swollen, embedded in his scalp. A nest of tick larvae must have fallen into his hair. It was spring, and the forest was full of the tiny parasites, waiting on leaves for a warm-blooded animal like a raccoon or a deer or a fifteen-year-old boy.

The boy knew how to deal with wood ticks. He wouldn't try to pull them out alive, the heads could break off and fester. He had to kill the ticks first by dabbing on nail polish remover from his mother's—

A little lapse there. Listen, there are lots of other ways to kill ticks, but you don't have what you need. You're just going to have to forget about it.

Until he made town, the boy would ignore the bloodsuckers. In the meantime, the best he could do was to take precautions.

Working around his shoulder sling, the boy pulled off his undershirt. The sun was weak but the hiking had warmed him and he didn't think he would miss it. He draped the fabric over his head, ripped a vine from the trunk of a mulberry tree, stripped the leaves, and knotted the circlet over the headdress. He must look like a shepherd in a Christmas play, but it would work.

Bare-chested, with his T-shirt draped on his head and his flannel shirt tied in a sling, the boy walked with a slight limp toward town.

I remember standing in front of the screen door, studying the handwritten sign that Roxanne McReynolds, the diner's owner, had nailed to the frame:

No shoes, no shirt, no service. And NO politics.

I cradled my football and sniffed under one arm. Circles of moisture stained my T-shirt, but the sign didn't say anything about an eleven-year-old's shirt being clean or odor-free.

Putting my face to the screen, I squinted to see if anyone was inside. The blinds were closed against the afternoon sun and the overhead fan was spinning. The benches were stacked upside down on the tables and Roxanne's nine-year-old daughter was pushing a huge string mop. Her name was Sky, and she was a couple of years behind me in school.

I went in the way I always did, stretching the screen door a little farther open on its coiled spring than necessary, then letting it pop closed with a bang.

Sky looked up but kept mopping. Braids, tied off with blue ribbons, framed her face.

"Hey," I said.

"Hey."

I sidestepped the damp spots on my way to the old deep-freeze, which had been recycled as an extra refrigerator for soft drinks. I put my football on the shelf over the coat rack, tipped the big lid back, and fanned the cold toward me. Then I pulled out a Dr. Pepper bottle, opened it, and took a swig. I closed the freezer, then hopped on top and watched Sky. She had rolled her overalls up at the ankles, but the stiff new denim still swamped her.

"So how come you're working so hard on a Saturday afternoon?" I asked.

She glanced back up at me. Her chin was quivering.

"Gosh, Sky, what's wrong?"

She shrugged and kept shoving the mop ahead of her. Wet, it must have weighed as much as she did.

"It's a pretty big job you got going there," I said. "You wanna take a break?"

She swiped at her eyes, then began to talk. "My mom went to Poteau to get supplies. Said she was gonna mop when she got back, but—" She stopped pushing the mop for the first time since I had come in and looked at me. "It's her birthday. I didn't want my mom mopping on her birthday."

It was sweet, but I didn't get why she was crying. "But why are you…upset?"

She swiped at her eyes again and went back to

shoving the mop. She looked exhausted. "This girl from my class was just in here. She said mopping the floor for somebody's birthday was the dumbest thing she ever heard of. And I'm thinkin' she might be right."

I leaned back and sipped my pop. "Well, this kid who was in here is obviously a lamebrain."

She looked at me.

"Sky, your mother's gonna love that you mopped this floor for her. Trust me."

"You really think so?" she asked shakily.

"Yeah, I really think so." I gulped the pop. "But your mom's birthday or not, if I'm gonna stay in here and drink this"—I tipped the bottle again—"then, for a while at least, you're going to have to put that thing down."

She raised one eyebrow in my direction.

"C'mon. I can't sit up here drinking Dr. Pepper with you mopping away in front of me."

"How come?"

I took a swig. "It makes me look bad."

She kept her eyes on her work, but a smile crossed her face.

I jumped off the freezer, took out another Dr. Pepper, opened it, and held it out to her. "Here, I'll pay. You can put it on my account."

"What account?"

"See, I knew you were gonna say that." I hopped back up on the freezer. "My account that you can open up for me as soon as you put down the mop."

This time she stopped working and looked at me when she smiled. I could see that some of her teeth were still coming in. She leaned the mop against the wall, put her hands on her hips, blew her bangs upward with her breath, and seemed to be thinking about my invitation. I scooted over, and she tiptoed to the freezer and climbed up.

"Thanks," she said, accepting the Dr. Pepper.

It had been easy talking to her as long as she was working, but now the only sound was the bump of her rubber soles kicking the front of the freezer as she drank her pop.

A set of wired-together deer antlers hung from a nail on the wall. I pointed with my bottle. "New antlers."

"Yeah."

"Nice."

"Thanks."

The chalkboard still listed the lunch special. Lamb fries, salad, dinner roll, and peach cobbler for $5.95. "Do you like lamb fries?" I asked her.

"No." She sipped her pop and bumped her shoes.

"Me neither." I took another drink. "Do you know what they are?"

She rolled her eyes. "Yes."

I scooted off the freezer and picked my way to the cash register. A drawing was fluttering on the wall next to a framed dollar bill. Roxanne always put Sky's drawings up, but I barely glanced at this one because I was looking at the photographs taped to the back of the cash register. The snapshots had been there as long as I could remember, but I had never paid much attention to them. Now, realizing that most of the pictures were of Sky, I studied them more closely.

There was a row of school portraits, one a year since kindergarten. And there were snapshots from when Sky was a baby and when she was a toddler. One faded Polaroid showed Roxanne, before she had any lines on her face, holding a newborn wrapped in a pale blue blanket. A dark-haired man with a mustache stood a few feet behind them.

"Who's the guy?" I asked.

Still kicking the freezer with the back of her shoes, Sky answered from across the room. "My father."

"So how come I've never seen him?" I leaned in to look at the man.

"Because he left three days after I was born."

"Oh." I moved on to another snapshot. "Well, at least you've got a picture of him. I don't have any pictures of me or my dad or my mom from when I was little."

"You don't?"

"Uh-uh."

The bumping stopped. "Why not?"

"Don't know. I asked my dad about it once. He said things can get lost when people move and then he changed the subject." I hoisted myself onto the counter. "It's what he always does when he doesn't want to talk to me about stuff."

Sky pulled her feet up and sat cross-legged. "Like

what kind of stuff?"

"Well, take today. Tony and me and my dad, we're passing the football around out on Main Street. My dad, he's teaching me about my stance, and so finally I ask him if he ever played on a team. He says most boys play a little football growing up and goes on talking to me about my form, and pretty soon I forgot that he never really answered my question."

Sky propped her elbows on the knees of her overalls and looked thoughtful. "Maybe your dad's got bad memories or somethin'. My mom never talks much about my father. Says it makes her sad."

I knew what she meant. My mother got sad sometimes, too. "Yeah," I said, "probably something like that. Parents. Go figure." I drained my Dr. Pepper and then pointed at the picture of Roxanne when she was younger. "Now your mom, she's cool in every way."

"She is?"

"Sure. She lets you wait tables. And carry plates of hot food and breakable dishes. It's like she trusts you to do important stuff even though you're little."

"I'm not *that* little."

"You know what I mean."

"Yeah." Sky sipped her pop. "I guess I do."

"I help in my dad's shop sometimes, but he won't let me work regular until I'm thirteen. He says I should have time to goof off and not be worrying about a job right now. But when I'm thirteen, he's gonna pay me and everything. Does your mom pay you?"

Sky shook her head. "Not exactly. But whenever

anything's left over at the end of the month, we put the money away for my college. My mom lets me write the deposit down in the book, and every time I do it, she tells me my dad left us the business so I could go off to school someday."

I looked at Sky and she looked straight back at me. "I know," she said after a moment. "Really, he just ran away. But I let her say it."

I slid down from the counter, walked in the dry spots over to the bucket, and took the mop in my hands. Sky jumped off the freezer.

"How long before your mom gets back?" I asked her.

She looked at the clock. "Maybe thirty minutes."

I surveyed how much of the floor was left to do. "Do you want the big job, putting the benches back down where the tile is dry, or the little job, finishing the mopping?"

She cocked her head to the side and put her hands on her hips. "Thanks," she said slowly, "but I think I want to do all of it."

"Oh, okay then." I handed her the mop. "I can see where you'd want to do that." I picked up the Dr. Pepper bottles and headed toward the door. "I'll throw these in the recycle bin," I said, "and bring you the money for the drinks tomorrow."

Already she was pushing the mop. "You know, you really don't have to pay for the Dr. Peppers. My mom lets me drink 'em for free."

"It's okay. I want to pay." I held the door open. "Do

you care if I let it bang?"

She looked up at me and grinned. "No. I do it, too."

Stepping out on the porch, I stretched the coil until the door was open all the way back, then let the frame fly shut with a loud thwack.

"Good one," she yelled.

I climbed over the railing, jumped off the porch, and jogged up the road, waving the bottles over my head to show I had heard.

Scraps

On April 19, 1995, at 9:02 a.m., on a morning filled with the promise of Spring, a bomb blast destroyed the nine-story Alfred P. Murrah Federal Building in downtown Oklahoma City. This, the largest act of domestic terrorism in our nation's history, claimed 168 lives, including 19 children, and wounded 674 people. Twenty-five buildings were severely damaged or destroyed and another 300 damaged. Cars near the building were set on fire. Glass, shattered from windows in a ten-block radius, filled the streets and sidewalks.

> — from "Alfred P. Murrah Federal Building Bombing, April 19, 1995: Final Report," The City of Oklahoma City, Oklahoma City Document Management Team, April 16, 1996, p. iii

"Expect more bombs."

> — from an announcement made to the press by Bob Fletcher, Militia of Montana spokesman, after the explosion of the Murrah Federal Building, quoted in Introduction to *False Patriots*, p. 3

"R-2, the second American Revolution, is coming."

> — Dan Shoemaker, militia organizer and the author of *The U.S. Militiaman's Handbook* ("a manual of how to engage and defeat government forces"), quoted in "Paramilitary Training: Militias Prepare for Confrontation with Government," *False Patriots*, p. 20

"It's the same as 1776, except the color of the coats are blue instead of red."

> — John Trochmann, head of Militia of Montana, quoted by Phil Bacharach in "Loose Cannons: A Cross-Section of the Militia Movement," *Oklahoma Gazette*, May 9, 1996 (vol. xviii, no. 19), p. 5

His Own Stupid Self

The boy knelt on the shore of Turtle Creek and scooped the fast-moving water with his hands. After he drank, he swished the liquid around in his mouth, then spit, trying to wash the acorn taste away. After many rinsings he sat back on his heels and studied the water.

Here, the river channel was full and the banks were steep. The cautious thing would be to find a narrower, more level spot to ford. But there was no predicting how far out of his way he would have to walk to find such a place. And he couldn't avoid a crossing by following the water all the way into Red Cedar. Turtle Creek meandered many miles through the hills before it wound back to town.

The boy checked over his shoulder. Not once had he seen or heard any sign of the Soldiers of God. But they were out there, he was sure, looking for him.

He slipped out of his hat and sling, stripped naked, then hesitated. If he left his boots on and the water was deep, it could be hard to swim even a few yards. On the other hand, it would be nearly impossible to keep his footing on the sharp rocks with his bare feet numbed by the cold water.

He put his boots on and tied up the rest of his clothes. It didn't take long to find a strong stick. Hooking the bundle over the end of it, he waded in.

At the shallow edges where the rocks had not been tumbled, the stones bit into his soles. He gasped as the water rose over the tops of his boots.

The current was swift, and by the time the stream was to his thighs he was using his stick as a staff. To keep track of how far the currents pushed him, he fixed his eyes on a dead post oak tree on the opposite bank. His lungs tightened as the water climbed his chest, and then there was a little drop-off. With a wince he sank to his neck.

He pushed off the bottom as well as he could, keeping his eyes fixed on the oak and raising his stick high. His progress was slow but steady. He was going to end up on the other side with blue lips and genitals the size of a peanut, but he would be safe, with dry clothes, and barely delayed. His muscles relaxed a bit against the cold and he breathed deep.

But there was no second deep breath, because at the moment it should have come, the boy caught movement, low, at eye level, and he turned to face a broad, tapered head.

He kicked and thrashed. He swam arm over arm, ignoring the ache in his shoulder, but his limbs were stiff and his boots were heavy. Only when he had his footing securely under him and the water was down to his waist did he dare look back.

There was no sign of the snake. But he had dropped his bundled clothes, and his right arm and shoulder were throbbing. With the water still up to his hips, he made his way toward the rocky bank. He was clambering out of the river, gasping, when a sharp pain pierced the inside of his thigh.

The boy plunged his hand into the stream and grabbed the head just behind the eyes and squeezed the sides of the mouth so that the bones cracked and the jaws slackened. He whipped the snake into the air and hurled it out over the river.

Don't panic. Panic spreads the venom.

"Don't panic, don't panic, don't panic," the boy chanted out loud, running the rest of the way up the slope. As if there were any way not to panic.

On dry land, he dropped to the rocks. He inspected the broken skin for fang punctures but couldn't tell if any of the tooth marks went that deep. He must have threatened the snake's nest. Otherwise it wouldn't have attacked like that.

The boy rubbed his temples and tried to remember his field guide. Harmless water snakes and poisonous cottonmouths, both, swam with their heads out of the water. But cottonmouths swam with their bodies on the surface while all species of simple water snakes kept their bodies under. Or was it the other way around?

It was elementary information, the kind any kid who grew up in southeastern Oklahoma would know, but the boy couldn't remember. Was it the panic, or the venom, already deadening his brain?

He closed his eyes and thought back. When he had first seen the snake, his gaze had been at water level. He wouldn't have seen the body on the surface even if it had been there. He would never know what kind of snake it was. But there was one thing he did know. His field guide said it. "If there is a possibility that a snake-bite is poisonous, seek medical attention immediately."

"IMMEDIATELY!" the boy shouted at the woods, swiping the air with his fist.

Naked except for his boots, squatting on the rocks with the razor-sharp edges cutting into his buttocks, the boy put his head in his hands and let his eyes fill. He should have looked for a shallower place to cross, a place where snakes would not nest and he would not have had to swim. He should have noted the reptile's coloring and scales and the way it carried its body, on top of the water or under. And he should *not* have shouted "Immediately!" just then. If the Soldiers of God found him because of that shout, maybe he deserved to be found.

Not true.

The Soldiers of God would be here soon. They had heard his panic and they would come. But they didn't need to come. It wasn't going to take the Soldiers of God to kill the boy. His own stupid self was doing a good job of that.

Scraps

The fiery end to the Branch Davidian compound in Waco, Texas, in April, 1993, is seared in the nation's memory. The tragic loss of life there was repeated two years later when Timothy McVeigh blew up the Oklahoma City federal building in what he indicated was an act of revenge.

> — from an editorial, "Grasping Waco's Lessons," *Christian Science Monitor*, Sept. 13, 1999, p. 10

Michael Fortier, McVeigh's friend, testified that McVeigh planned to bomb the Oklahoma City federal building "because that was where the orders for the attack on Waco came from."

> — Tom Lindley, "Oklahoma Can't Escape Waco's Fallout," *Daily Oklahoman*, Sept. 28, 1999, p. 9-A

After denying for years that federal agents used incendiary devices in the raid, FBI Director Louis Freeh acknowledged that two pyrotechnic tear-gas canisters were indeed fired at the compound. The news sent the FBI into a protective crouch—and infuriated antigovernment activists who have long believed the Feds covered up the truth about Waco. Few law-enforcement operations have spurred as many conspiracy theories—or resonated as deeply with those Americans who are profoundly distrustful of the government.

> — Michael Isikoff, "The Waco Flame-Up," *Newsweek*, Sept. 6, 1999, p. 30

I remember the first time I fired a sniper rifle. I was twelve, and Tony and I had biked out to the quarry swimming hole.

My mother still wouldn't let us swim there unless an adult was with us, but she didn't have to be the adult anymore, and in the middle of summer there were usually people around. Today didn't look promising, though. The temperature was one hundred and twelve and there were no bicycles or motorcycles parked at the picnic tables.

We left our bikes in the shade so the seats wouldn't be scorching when we were ready to leave. Already shirtless, we kicked off our shoes and started up the trail that led into the high rocks, hoping to see someone below when we emerged above the water.

I walked onto the ledge of the diving cliff. The lake was so clear I could see the cratered floor and the shadows the clouds made against it, passing over. Years ago, some teenagers had floated a dock out in the middle of the water, and it swayed, deserted. No towels were spread on the pebble beach. No six-packs were lodged in the shallow. The only living creatures were a clan of turtles, languishing on floating logs.

"Man, don't tell me we rode all the way out here in this heat for nothing," I said to Tony.

"You realize, a' course," Tony answered, "that your mom would never know if we swam."

I looked at him.

"Seriously," he went on. "It's not like we're alone. You're watching me and I'm watching you. Not to mention, we're the best swimmers in—"

A shot rang out and echoed off the rocks. We ducked and looked around, then dropped to our knees as another shot followed and then another.

We traded glances and leaned slowly out over the ledge. All of the turtles had disappeared. We looked back into the woods.

"There," Tony said, pointing.

Behind the treeline, someone lay on his belly with a scoped rifle propped on a bipod and his eye to the sight.

"I never saw anybody turtle-shoot with a sniper rifle before," Tony whispered. "Only shotguns. Or once, maybe, a pistol."

We held still until the gunman stood up, walked out from behind the birches, and looked up at our ledge.

"Taliferro!" we yelled, waving from the high rocks. "Sean Taliferro!"

He called us over, and barefoot, we picked our way down the face of the rocks.

Red-faced, Sean yelled as we walked up, "Didn't you see the tape?" Sean Taliferro was one of the most easygoing people I knew. I had never seen him angry before.

We looked behind us and saw that where the beach began, "Do Not Cross" police tape had been strung between the trees. Since we had approached the swimming hole by the trail over the rocks, we had detoured around the beach. Tony and I looked at each other sheepishly.

Sean shook his head, scouted the rocks again, and when he was convinced that there weren't any more of us, seemed to relax a bit. "So," he said. "You boys are spending your summer loafing instead of practicing football." Sean had quarterbacked for the Red Cedar high school team in the sixties.

"Oh, we're playin' some ball," Tony answered distractedly. We were peeking around Sean, eyeing his gun.

"It's a Sako TRG-21," he said, walking back into the trees and squatting beside the rifle. "Finnish-made. Serious equipment."

We followed and knelt down beside him.

"But why are you shooting turtles," I asked, "when you could use the range at the base camp?"

Sean dusted a red felt rag lightly over the gun. "The target range is good for lots of things, but a shooter needs to practice in real conditions."

Tony and I kept our eyes on the gun.

Sean chuckled. "Want to try?" he asked.

"Are you kidding?" Tony blurted, his eyes wide.

Tony went first. The distance for his hand to reach from the proper position to the trigger was too far, so Sean showed him how to adjust it. Sean took eight Winchester .308 rounds and gave four to Tony and put four aside for me. The turtles were gone now, so Tony shot at the dock.

"Come with your grandfather to range practice sometime," Sean told him. "There's a lot I could teach you."

Then he looked at me. "You, on the other hand, having been taught by your dad, one of the best shots I know—" Sean looked around. "—need a more advanced target." He pointed out across the water. "What about the farthest sign?"

After a long-ago drowning the county had dotted the quarry with warnings. The most distant "SWIM AT YOUR OWN RISK" sign was stuck on a rusted pole on the opposite side of the lake. I held my hand to my eyes. I knew from swimming across to the sign that the metal was already pocked with old bullet holes.

"First we'll position the rig together," Sean said. "That way you can learn."

Sean showed me how to click the legs into place on the bipod, and explained how the spiked feet grabbed the ground. He said that the rifle was mounted with a Tasco Titan scope, which was not normally a tactical sight but was the only scope he had on hand with a thirty millimeter tube. "It will do all you need it to," he told me.

Sean spread a towel out over the leaves. I got down on my belly and fixed a rag between my naked shoulder and the butt pad. He showed me how the bolt handle and knob were big enough for a firm hold, and the way that the mechanism moved forward and backward with "total smoothness."

He fit my finger and thumb into the pistol grip grooves and made sure the swells were fixed under my hand. I adjusted my body for the most solid feel and took aim.

The bullet holes in the sign were crisp circles in my sight. I picked a spot, hoping to dot the "I" in "RISK."

Sean talked in low tones about how a gun's trigger pull could be too heavy or too light, and how the factory setting of three point five pounds was just right for him on this gun. "It is a pressure at which the shooter can be deliberate but not distracted," he said.

"Deliberate but not distracted," I repeated to myself.

"This particular pull"—Sean went on talking to Tony behind me—"feels like velvet." Then Sean stopped whispering and the two of them held still.

I thought "velvet" was an odd word for a trigger. I took several breaths and exhaled slowly. At the end of the final breath, I pulled the trigger. "Velvet" was exactly right.

Little Red Riding Hood
Meets Wolfman

The boy didn't spend much time on the creek bank crying. He stood up and wiped his eyes and changed his plans.

His bundled clothes had snagged downstream. He retrieved the undershirt that had served as his hat and ripped it in two. One piece of cloth he wrapped above the snakebite, the other he wrapped below, trying not to look at the bruise spreading across his thigh. His jeans were tight even when dry and he couldn't fit them on over the bandage, so for pants he had only his soggy briefs, but soggy briefs were better than no briefs.

Instead of fixing the sling, he tied the sleeves of his wet flannel shirt around his hips, hoping to hide the fact that he was wearing only underwear. Then he rolled his jeans and belt into a ball, stuffed them under his good arm, and squished off toward the highway in his soaked boots, cradling his right side to take the weight off his shoulder and checking behind him with each spongy step.

—

From behind the trees, the boy studied Highway 259. He crouched for what seemed like an eternity without seeing a single car. He was scared about the bite.

So scared that you're going to come out of the woods and stand on the shoulder and put your thumb in the air when any car that comes by could be militia? You're scared enough to do that?

He was scared enough to do that. He was dizzy. And sick to his stomach. It could be the sun, the hiking with no food, but he really did think it was a cottonmouth.

What are the odds of that? How many people do you know who were ever bitten by a cottonmouth?

None, the boy thought. Because they were all dead.

If you're making jokes, you're probably all right.

He wasn't trying to be funny.

Are you sure hitching is the answer? You seemed so against it this morning.

This morning the boy wasn't snakebit. Besides, hitching might even be a better plan because in five minutes he would be in town. Roxanne, or his dad if he were there, could drive him to the Poteau emergency room.

The boy knelt and bent his head and folded his hands and began to pray.

Stop that and get up. A car is coming.

From between the trees, the boy watched a Cadillac speed toward him. Too expensive to be militia, he thought, but he didn't act fast enough and the car sped by.

A Winnebago approached. He remembered a Soldier of God driving over from Wilburton in a Winnebago once, so he stayed put.

It was a long time before another vehicle appeared over the rise. When one did, it was a Dodge minivan.

No minivans, he told himself. Period.

Then, finally, behind the minivan, a station wagon with bikes on top, pulling a boat. Hardly anybody who lived in southeastern Oklahoma drove a foreign car. And bikes, and a boat? It was probably some family headed out to see the Runestone, or Robbers' Cave, or to ride Cavanal Hill. There were lots of places a Volvo station wagon with bikes and a boat could be heading to or from on a beautiful day like today.

Carrying his jeans over his arm to hide his underwear, the boy walked quickly to the asphalt shoulder and waved his hand in the air.

Through the tinted glass he could see two people. The woman was driving and the man was reading a map.

"Come on, people," the boy said under his breath. "Come on. Pull over…"

What if the Volvo didn't stop? What if nobody who looked trustworthy stopped? Not that he would blame them. He didn't look very trustworthy himself.

Another car appeared in the distance. His view of it was partially blocked by the Volvo's bikes and boat, but he could see that it was some old junkmobile.

This is not good.

"Come on, people, come on and stop…please."

The boy's waves at the station wagon became frantic. It had been edging over, as if to check him out. The man put his map down and looked at the boy. But when the boy started motioning wildly, the car moved back to the center of its lane and crept by.

"No! Please!" the boy shouted, limping after the station wagon.

The Volvo kept going, slowly, as if the driver was wondering what to do, then began to pick up speed.

The boy turned around and squinted to see if there was a tag on the front of the oncoming car. No, but Oklahoma didn't require a plate on the front, so it might mean nothing. On the other hand, it could mean militia. Lots of militiamen thought license plates were a government conspiracy. The boy considered. It would look very odd if he went back into the woods.

Who cares how it would look? Just pretend you never came out here waving and yelling, and disappear back into the forest. Go now. Fast.

But if they were militia, they had already seen him. And besides, he felt weak and feverish. Images of a hospital bed in a sterile room with fresh, turned-down linens filled his head, and he stood his ground.

There were two men in the front seat. The one on the passenger side was wearing a red hunter's cap with the fur flaps flipped up. As the car pulled over, the boy read the stickers on the front windshield. "4-H." "FFA." "Ask me about my honor student." Maybe this was going to be okay.

The glass cranked down and the bill of the hunter's

cap poked out of the window. The eyes under it squinted up at the boy. "What happened to you, son?" the man asked.

"I'm snakebit, sir. I wrapped my leg and now I can't get my jeans back on."

The man turned to the driver and the two exchanged looks.

This is no good. Just say thanks, you're sorry, you made a mistake, and wave them—

"Where are y'all headed?" the boy asked, cutting off the voice in his head.

"Heavener."

The boy knew they were local from the way the man put the heavy accent on "Heave." Heavener was north, on the other side of the Ouachita National Forest. "Could I ride as far as Red Cedar?"

"Of course you can ride as far as Red Cedar," the man in the hunter's cap answered. "But if you're snakebit, you ought to let us take you on to the hospital."

"Thanks, but Red Cedar will do."

The man in the hunter's cap shrugged, then got out of the car and banged his boot against the back door. "You have to kick it to pop the handle," he explained. The door swung open and the crackle of radio static came from inside.

Not a good sign.

It was only a CB. Everybody had them.

Especially everybody in the militia.

The man held the door open as the boy climbed in, then shut it firmly behind him. It was dark because instead of a rear window there was cardboard held in with tape. Springs poked the boy, and foam stuffing was pouring out of a split in the upholstery. There was a cardboard box on the floor packed with a thermos, ready-to-eat meals, and boxes of 12-gauge shotgun shells. The boy remembered that turkey hunting season had opened.

"Out turkey hunting?" he asked the driver.

"Right," the man said, keeping his eyes forward.

They were just two guys out to shoot their one bird each and they were going to deliver the boy to the diner's screen door and in five minutes he'd be home free. Surely.

It's too late now anyway.

The boy looked for a seat belt. As if after everything he'd been through he should be worried about a seat belt. There wasn't one. It could be because the car predated seat belts. Or it could be because seat belts were another conspiracy.

Without looking to see if any cars were coming, the driver pulled onto the highway and sped up. Already going fast, they pulled around the station wagon. As the boy passed by, the lady smiled and waved, apparently relieved that someone had stopped for him.

For the first time the driver looked over his shoulder and smiled at the boy. His right and left incisors were capped in gold. "So you're headed to Red Cedar?"

"Yes, sir."

"Don't mind if we take a little detour first, do you?"

"Well, sir. Actually, sir. I don't mean to impose, but I'm feeling sick and I really need to get home."

"Understood. But we've got one stop to make before we hit town. It'll only take a sec."

The car slowed and pulled toward the edge. The driver made a sharp U-turn, laying rubber across the dashed line and throwing the boy against the door. The boy's heart thumped wildly. He didn't try to calm it. If venom was pumping through his veins, it was the least of his problems now.

They passed the Volvo again, now going in the opposite direction. The boy looked for a handle to roll down the window but it was broken off, so he waved at the woman with both hands, trying to signal for help. The lady watched them go by and waved back, a confused look on her face.

The driver with the gold incisors picked his CB mike up off the clip. "Wolfman, coming in with Little Red Riding Hood. Over and out." He clipped the mike back.

The boy tried to swallow but ended up gulping air.

Grabbing a pack of Lucky Strikes off the dash, the driver flicked up a cigarette. With no break in speed, the other man reached over and steered with one finger while the driver lit a match, puffed, squeezed the match out, then tucked the matchbook into the cellophane.

"You look a little nervous," the driver said, a cigarette dangling from lips as he watched the boy in the cracked rear-view mirror.

The boy didn't answer. He felt sick.

"Here. Take the last of my smokes." The driver handed the Lucky Strikes over the seat. "A cigarette will calm you down."

The boy accepted the nearly empty package but made no move to take out a cigarette.

"Go ahead," the driver said, his eyes locked on the boy. "I don't think you're going to have to worry about cancer."

The man in the hunter's cap stifled a chuckle. The boy turned to him, and tried to keep the fear out of his voice. "Is Little Red Riding Hood your, uh, CB handle?"

"Come on, you're smarter than that, son," the man answered. He plucked his hat off by the bill, reached over into the back seat, and fitted the cap firmly onto the boy's head. "Little Red Riding Hood is the one who just came in outta the woods."

I remember aiming footballs through the tractor tire that hung from the swing set frame in our side yard.

Earlier that year, when I turned thirteen, I had started working in my dad's antique store. But that afternoon my father had pronounced that nobody should work on a beautiful Saturday in October, and the two of us had pulled the card tables stacked with hand-me-down clothes and used baby toys back inside the store. Now my parents were stretched out on one of the rag rugs my mother had sewn, playing cards under our big elm tree. It was what they always did when they had something important to talk about.

Pet was four years old, young enough to think that each time I threw the ball it was for her benefit, and she sat with her eyes on me, waiting for the next pass. I bent to rub her belly and she rolled over, still wagging her tail. That was when I noticed Sky walking up the road from the diner. Wearing faded blue overalls, cut off and frayed at the knees, she angled across the grass in my direction.

"I was wonderin'," she said, coming up. "Would you mind if I sat on your porch?" She adjusted the big canvas bag on her shoulder that she carried everywhere, even to school. "I've been wanting to draw Roy Roye's place, and that would be the best angle."

I looked across to the Royes'. A crack in the kitchen window was taped. The yard was clay, the grass rubbed off by a skinny greyhound pacing up and down a chain link fence. The garden was overgrown and motorcycle parts rusted in the driveway. I must have looked at her kind of funny, but all I said was, "Sure, no problem." I went back to my throwing, hoping for my passes to hit their mark in a way that I hadn't before.

An hour later, I was bent in half with fatigue, Pet was asleep in a pile of leaves, and my parents had long ago rolled up the rug and gone in. But Sky was still on our porch steps with her sketch pad propped on her scuffed-up knees.

"Can I look?" I asked as I walked over.

"I don't mind."

I plodded up the steps and knelt behind her. I blinked and leaned over her shoulder, my eyes going back and forth between the lot across the street and her drawing of it.

There *were* pumpkins on that vine in the garden, and a whirligig tucked into the weeds. And that line of honey jars was just visible along the front kitchen sill. I cleared my throat and sat down next to her. "You're really good."

"Thanks."

"How'd you learn?" I asked, unbuckling my ankle weights.

She shrugged, shading the pumpkins with the side of her lead. "I don't know. Mostly I've just always been able to do it." She had two extra pencils in her free hand and she kept switching them around. "My mom checks out art books and drawing books for me from the library." Poteau was the nearest real library, forty-five minutes away. "Some of them help."

"Your picture," I said, pointing across the street with the tip of the football, "is better than the real thing."

She stopped sketching, looked at me, and raised one eyebrow. "My picture *is* the real thing."

Man, she was an interesting kid. "It's cool to be so into something," I said, my voice trailing off as I watched her draw.

Once she spit on her finger and rubbed smudges into the paper. Another time she used her T-shirt. Finally, she signed her name in the upper corner. The letters had an offhand, stylized look that must have taken a lot of practice.

"You know, I never told you before, but I think it's nice—" I pointed with the football again, to her signature. "Your name. It's kind of, you know, poetic. Good name for an artist."

Her blue eyes looked straight at me. "My mom says that, too."

"So, you're like"—I turned the football in my hands—"named for a famous artist, or something?"

"No…" She hesitated, as if wondering whether she should go on. "My mom named me that," she said finally, flipping the page over in her sketch pad and starting a new drawing, "because the sky goes forever in every direction with nothing in the way."

It was quiet for a long time—her drawing, me watching—until Vince and Shelly Williams's pickup raised a cloud of dust, passing by in front of us. We followed the truck with our eyes as it pulled up in the diner parking lot.

Sky started packing and organizing her bag. Pencil tins. Spiral rings filled with curled pages. Charcoals. Pastels. Sponges and rags.

Two blocks away, the screen door opened and closed and Roxanne came down the steps of the diner porch, whipping her dishtowel over her head. Sky jumped up and waved to her mother, then slung her bag over her shoulder and faced me. She hadn't packed her sketch pad.

"I've got something for you," she said, tearing a page out of the tablet. She smiled, and I noticed that recently she had gotten braces. She handed me the paper and hurried away.

I almost dropped my football. Looking back at me from the drawing was a square-jawed boy. Brows knitted and bangs needing a trim, his eyes focused on a point off the page. The proportions weren't perfect, but there was something about the sketch that exactly captured the feeling of getting set, hunkering back, and cocking an arm to whip the ball on its arc.

"Gosh—" I looked up, but she was already halfway to the diner. Her hair swung loose and unbrushed halfway down her back, and her legs were long and skinny. "Thanks," I said softly.

I watched until she disappeared behind the screen door, which she shut quietly behind her, then went back to studying the drawing. She had even gotten my fingers right, splayed across the laces. She must know a lot about football, I thought. Or maybe she didn't know anything about football. Maybe she just saw things.

Scraps

Elohim City lies at the end of six and a half miles of the worst dirt road in eastern Oklahoma. If you show up there unannounced and tell the guards you're lost, they will know you're lying—there is no other possible destination....

This is exactly the way the Rev. Robert Millar planned it. When Millar, a former Mennonite from Canada, and a handful of followers founded the community in 1972, they situated it high on a hill so they can see who is coming long before the visitors arrive.

... [T]his community of less than 100 residents has been the center of intense media scrutiny for much of the last year after it was revealed Elohim City, and Millar in particular, has ties to some fringe groups advocating the overthrow of the government and likely had attracted the interest of federal building bombing suspect Timothy McVeigh.

— George Lang, "Welcome to Elohim City," *Oklahoma Gazette*, March 28, 1996 (vol. xviii, no. 13), p. 4

WASHINGTON (Reuters)—FBI agents arrested seven

West Virginia militia members or sympathizers Friday on charges of plotting to blow up the bureau's fingerprint records complex and transporting explosive materials....

The FBI said the inquiry involv[ed] Floyd Raymond Looker, the West Virginia militia's self-described "commanding general"....

Federal agents were able to infiltrate the group through a cooperating witness, who was a close associate of Looker....

Looker...has said he made his living as a preacher and a lawyer....

— "Militia Members, Supporters Charged in Bombing Scheme," *Daily Oklahoman*, Oct. 12, 1996, p. 5

Full Circle

Somebody banged the side of the car, and the doors of the old Pontiac swung open from the outside. Curled in the back seat, the boy lifted his eyes to the barrel of an M-16. Another M-16 was at the opposite door.

"Let's go," ordered the soldier closest to the boy's head, motioning with his weapon. It was Vince Williams. Vince and his wife, Shelly, were colonels in the militia.

"Colonel Vince," the boy whispered. As in the armed forces, Soldiers of God were called by their rank paired with their last names, but to tell the Colonels Williams apart, an exception was made. "Sir, I'm snakebit."

Colonel Vince called to his wife, who appeared by his side. "Says he's snakebit," Colonel Vince told her.

Colonel Shelly told the boy to hang his legs out the door, then unwrapped the rags from his thigh. Her fingers were gentle. "What kind of snake?" she asked, examining the punctures.

"Cottonmouth."

"You sure?"

The boy lifted his head off the seat. "Yard long, dark back, light belly." He quoted whatever details he could remember from his books, though he had observed none of it. "Vertical slits for pupils, triangulated head, venom sacs." Maybe the Soldiers of God would leave him alone if they thought he was going to die anyway.

"How long ago?"

He let his head wobble back on the foam stuffing. Seemed like a year. "Two hours, maybe," he said.

She crawled between the seats. "I doubt it was a cottonmouth or the wound would be more purple and swollen by now." She unzipped her fanny pack, shook a thermometer out, and stuck it in his mouth. "This'll hurt some," she said, already cleaning the bite. "And I'm fresh outta tearjerkers."

Managing a limp smile, the boy sat up. As the three minutes lapsed, Colonel Shelly finished cleaning the wound, then took the boy's blood pressure and listened to his heartbeat and breathing. She withdrew the thermometer and studied it, then put an elastic band above the bite and taped on gauze.

"Thank you," the boy said weakly.

"Don't thank me. You ought to have an extractor and a shot of anti-venom and an I.V. just to be sure." She backed out of the door. "I'm not doin' none of that."

The boy's stomach turned over. "I think I'm gonna be sick."

"So?" Another soldier pointed his M-16 at the boy's head.

When the boy saw who it was, his gut lurched again. "Tony—"

"We don't give out vomit bags," the soldier said. "And it's Private Rossetti to you."

The boy scooted toward the open door. He hung his torso out of the car and vomited bile. The hunter's cap fell off his head and into the dust.

"You're better now. Terrific." Private Rossetti motioned with his gun. "Better enough to visit headquarters."

Headquarters. Already.

"Move!"

"I can't move."

Private Rossetti kicked the car tire, his boot landing an inch from the boy's face.

The boy's head jerked up.

"See? I was sure you could move."

The boy dragged himself out of the vehicle and struggled to his hands and knees. He stood up woozily, still dressed in his underwear and boots with his flannel shirt tied at his hips. That was when he saw it wasn't just the Williamses and Private Rossetti standing guard over him. The boy and the Pontiac were ringed by a dozen soldiers in the middle of the base camp assembly yard. He was going to be sick again.

Stop it. Now. If you're going to get out of here in anything other than a body bag, you have to pull yourself together. You're no stranger here. Use what you know.

One thing he knew was that if the soldiers had been ordered to shoot on sight he would be dead already, so that order had not been given. His stomach un-cramped a bit at the thought. He took a deep breath and tried to stand a little straighter.

Colonel Shelly stepped through the line and handed him a set of camo pants and shirt. If the circumstances had been different he could have hugged her for that, but "thank you" was all he said.

He untied the wet knot of flannel and tossed his shirt in the car. Shaking out the starched trousers, he saw they were baggy enough to fit over his bandaged leg. He began to dress, moving his eyes around the circle as he did so. Acknowledging each soldier with a nod, he tried to take in everything.

At twelve o'clock, dead ahead by the dinner bell, Sean Taliferro stood with his rifle. Taliferro had grown up in Red Cedar. He had cut short his high school foot-ball career to go to Vietnam, which was where he had learned to snipe.

One o'clock. Cherry Martindale, the boy's old Sunday school teacher, had charcoaled her eyes. Martindale rescued strays from the Poteau pound, and Pet had been one of her special finds. The boy won-dered if she knew what had happened to his dog.

Two o'clock. Jim Redhawk, Tony's grandfather, his T-shirt proclaiming him a "Prayer Warrior," stood with his hands folded in front of him. Redhawk claimed to be a victim of Gulf War Disease, but the army disput-ed it. In spite of his shaking hands he was the best darts player in LeFlore County.

Three o'clock. Old Davis Johns held an open Bible.

Johns raised fighting cocks and made so much money in gaming that he owned a good portion of LeFlore County. Over Johns's shoulder was the farmhouse, the militia's headquarters and the meeting place for services. The boy scanned the dark windows and sagging porches for any signs of movement, but saw none.

Four and five o'clock. Ronald and Johnny Murry held their guns at port arms. The Murry twins owned a dairy which they left to their manager to run so they could spend their time playing foosball at the Game Room and Lounge. They lived in a tidy house on Hill Street with a woman they both claimed to be married to. The second marriage was illegal, but the law left them alone.

"He's stallin', Colonel," someone shouted.

Colonel Shelly waved them off. "I guess we got time for him to put some pants on. 'Sides which," she said, just to the boy, "I think you got a right to see who's been hunting you."

Six o'clock. Coach Scotty, the high school football coach, tipped his "Bucks" cap and the boy saluted back. Scotty Thomas had been an assistant coach at the University of Oklahoma until he was arrested in an after-game brawl and was convicted for assault.

Seven and eight o'clock. Jake and Ricardo Lucero, father and son, stood in at-ease position, the butts of their rifles in the dust. The Luceros were quiet men who kept to themselves; the boy didn't see them much even though they lived next door to him. Jake had lost an arm in Nam, and hand-lettered around his headband were the words "VC Hunting Club." In his professional wrestling days he had been known as the One-Armed Avenger. Ricardo was rumored to be a genius. He spent his time watching television and reading *Soldier of Fortune*.

Nine o'clock. Roy Roye, who lived across the road from the boy, had attached a bayonet to his M-16. Roy owned the Game Room and Lounge and rebuilt motorcycles. A few years ago, after the boy took that bad fall behind the Git 'N Go, Roy had fixed his wrecked bike. Roy said it was his way of trying to repay the boy's mother for giving him reading lessons.

Ten o'clock. Wolfman, backdropped by the old round barn thirty yards in the distance. He must not be from these parts because the boy had never seen him before today. Wolfman accepted a cigarette from Roy Roye and grinned at the boy between drags, gold caps sparkling. The boy was moving on when a memory crossed his mind and his gaze jumped over Wolfman and landed back on the barn.

When he was little, the boy had visited another round barn. His father had tapped on the wall, explaining that it was Morse code, and had shown his son how he could hear the tapping clearly from any point on the perimeter. The boy had been more excited about the code than the acoustics. It was the first time he realized his father knew things like that.

But that other barn, painted and restored, was nothing like the barn behind Wolfman. This barn was tilting, with rotted slats popping loose and not much paint left to flake. It held the soldiers' stockpile of ammo and explosives, but except for the padlock on the door, anyone who didn't know would take it for abandoned, which was the intended effect ...

Colonel Shelly put her hand on the boy's shoulder and joggled him. "Stalling won't change anything," she said.

He wasn't stalling, he was studying.

She offered the boy a piece of old rope, and he realized that he had stopped dressing. "Here," she said. "Hitch your pants. No fashion statements allowed." She was trying to put him at ease. He took the rope and completed his inspection as he threaded it through the loops.

Eleven o'clock. Wolfman's friend held an Uzi submachine gun in the crook of his elbow while he pulled on a pair of fingerless black knit gloves.

The boy caught his breath at the sight of the gloves. They were like the gloves that had inspected his mother's body. The soldier waved, then spit a wad of tobacco juice in the direction of the boy's feet. The boy considered the man, the hands, and the gloves— but it was impossible to know.

Twelve o'clock. Full circle to Taliferro and the dinner bell.

Dressed, the boy slipped his boots on, and Colonel Shelly told him to fall in. But the boy's attention had skipped back to Wolfman, puffing.

"Please, just a second. I want to get my clothes and cigarettes." He glanced at Coach Scotty as he ducked into the car, wishing he could explain. He didn't smoke, but the cigarettes might help him befriend someone who did. He dropped the Lucky Strikes into the pocket of his camo shirt and bundled his discarded garments.

"Listen, kid." Colonel Vince stuck his head in the car after him. "Time's up. Way past up."

Colonel Shelly inspected the boy's jeans, belt, flannel shirt, and torn T-shirt. Then she handed the clothes back to him. Private Rossetti stepped into position behind him and the Colonels Williams took places in front. The boy picked up the hunter's cap that had fallen off his head when he vomited, and dusted it off. He walked over to Wolfman and gave him the hat.

"Thanks, Red," Wolfman said.

The boy tipped his chin, then fell back into line. Colonel Vince ordered, "Forward," and the little formation moved across the assembly yard and into headquarters.

Scraps

Patriot groups increasingly overlap with the 474 race- or ethnicity-based "hate groups" that were documented in 1997 by the Intelligence Project.

— "'Patriot' Numbers Decrease, But Movement Gets Meaner,"
SPLC Report, June 1998 (vol. 28, no. 2), p. 1

"And we're not necessarily 100-percent white—I've got a little Indian blood. But basically we're white separatists. We're not supremacists. I believe a black man is just as equal as a white man—among his own people. A yellow man is just as equal—in his own people."

— Robert McKenry of Elohim City, quoted in *Oklahoma Gazette*, March 28, 1996 (vol. xviii, no. 13), p. 6

"Do you believe that Africans, Mexicans, Arabs, or Asians could have created America? One look at their squalid, collectivist, regional pest holes is the obvious answer."

— Sergeant First Class Steven M. Barry, paramilitary underground figure and editor of *The Resister*, quoted by Gregory A. Walker in "'A Defector in Place': Special Forces Underground," SPLC's *Intelligence Report*, Summer 1999 (issue 95), p. 11

I, as a free Aryan man, hereby swear an unrelenting oath upon the green graves of our sires, upon the children in the wombs of our wives, upon the throne of God almighty, sacred is His name, to join together in holy union with those brothers in this circle and to declare forthright that from this moment on I have no fear of death, no fear of foe; that I have a sacred duty to do whatever is necessary to deliver our people from the Jew and bring total victory to the Aryan race.

> — from the oath of The Order, a paramilitary extremist group, quoted in *Gathering Storm*, p. 140

Dear White Patriots:

... All 5,000 White Patriots are now honor bound and duty bound to pick up the sword and do battle against the forces of evil. Swear you'll not put down your sword until total victory is ours.... Let the blood of our enemies flood the streets, rivers, and fields of the nation, in Holy vengeance and justice.... The following point system for Aryan warriors of The Order [for each kill]: Niggers (1), White race traitors (10), Jews (10), Judges (50).... Let the battle axes swing smoothly and the bullets whiz true.

> — from a declaration signed by "Glenn Miller, loyal member of 'The Order,'" quoted in *Gathering Storm*, pp. 98–99

I remember looking down at my legs to see if the quivering was visible.

It was early August, and I was late to work at my father's antique store because I had just finished my first practice with the high school football team. Coach Scotty had invited me to drill with the varsity squad— a big deal for a fourteen-year-old freshman—and workouts ran from seven to ten a.m., so it was mid-morning by the time I got to the shop.

As I came in the back door, my dad was studying the county newspaper. "Cherry Martindale has a sale going this weekend," he said without looking up. "Would you like to handle it for me?" He put the paper down. "You did a good job last week in Octavia. That old Fiesta Ware is worth something."

I liked scouting garage sales and my dad had started letting me negotiate my own prices and trades. "Sure," I said, slumping into an old church pew the two of us planned to refinish. "Absolutely."

I was exhausted. I guess it was obvious, because my father looked over his reading glasses. He studied me with a slight smile on his face. "How'd practice go?"

"I'll probably live another hour."

He chuckled. "Good. Because I've got a job for you and it'll take about that long." He motioned toward the front of the store. I reached over the back of the pew and parted the beaded curtain.

Mrs. Davis Johns was pawing through my mother's brightly colored rag rugs, sewn from the old clothes and linens my dad and I bought for pennies and from our own family's scraps. The Johnses lived in the biggest house in the county, and I had never seen her in the store before.

"She's going to take the armoire," my father said. He called it an armoire, but really it was just an old pine cabinet. For as long as I could remember, the piece had stood in the corner of the little house I had helped my dad paint and trim and convert into the antique shop. "Do you think you could clean it up before you expire?"

"Okay." I pulled myself up, tested my legs, and stepped through the rattling beads as I waved. "Hi, Mrs. Johns." My father followed me into the front room, and the two of them began to negotiate.

Hands on hips, I surveyed the contents of the cabinet, all of it blanketed with a fine layer of dust. A bandanna that I had kept wet with fresh water during practice was tied around my forehead. I unknotted the cloth and began to unload the shelves, ragging each item off as I set it aside. Used postcards. Knitted potholders. A Cherokee dreamcatcher, "Made in Korea."

Old books and magazines filled the bottom shelves. I pulled the stacks out and sorted them into piles. The last volume was an oversized leather scrapbook. I ran my bandanna over the dusty cover, revealing a gold script monogram embossed on the front. "LeF." I stood up.

My father and Mrs. Johns were still dickering at the counter. I waited for them to finish, flipping through the pages of the book. Small black corners had been mounted for every picture and keepsake, but all of the mementos had been removed. I turned the album over. A sticker said "$1."

Mrs. Johns's red nails began to click through a deck of credit cards, and my father finally looked over at me.

I held up my find. "What's this?"

He shrugged. "Somebody's old scrapbook we're re-selling."

"It's not *somebody's* old scrapbook, Dad, look. It's got the same initials as Mom's dishes."

My father left Mrs. Johns holding the credit card out to him and threaded his way to me through the aisles. He took the album from my hands.

I pointed to the monogram.

My dad turned every page, closed the book, and headed back to the cash register with it.

"Dad—"

"Not now, son."

"Excuse me?" I said to his back.

My father put the scrapbook in the drawer under the counter and turned to me. "Not *now*, son." His eyebrows knitted and his forehead creased. He looked straight at me and his eyes were intense.

Mrs. Johns looked back and forth between the two of us, her credit card still in the air. My father took the card and swiped it through the machine, and Mrs. Johns went back to chattering. She was going to have the legs cut off the cabinet, add a wine rack, install a refrigerator …

My father picked up a tape measure and followed her to the parking lot.

I draped my bandanna over my shoulder, went to the drawer, and took out the scrapbook. Once, it must have been expensive. The endpapers were a burnished gold.

My father was back, standing in front of me. "The armoire won't fit in her Suburban," he said. "I need you to deliver it."

All the kids in Red Cedar drove before they turned sixteen and I was used to running errands in my dad's truck, but I didn't answer him.

"Could you get the dolly from the back room, please?"

I stood still. "What does 'L,E,F' stand for?"

My father looked at me a minute, then disappeared through the beads. When he came back, he was pushing the dolly.

"Dad, it's not a hard question."

Bringing the dolly flush to the armoire, my father

motioned me to the other side of it. He rolled up his sleeves, exposing the fish and guns tattoo, and I took my place opposite him. Counting to three, we hoisted the furniture onto the dolly. The two of us stood back, breathing hard.

"You know," I said, "I have never seen any old pictures of our family."

My father ran his hands over the wood grain of the cabinet. "Mrs. Johns is going to cut up an old and beautiful thing."

"Please, Dad. Don't change the subject."

"I'm not changing the subject because there isn't a subject." He leaned in close to the pine, as if to smell it. "I'm just wondering if I made a mistake, letting her buy this old piece."

"Is there a reason, Dad? Why I haven't ever seen any pictures?"

He kept his eyes on the wood.

"Or an old high school yearbook? Or an old college T-shirt? Or yours and Mom's wedding pictures? Or even a baby picture of *me*?"

"I bought this armoire out of the Luceros' barn."

"I mean, maybe you threw your stuff away, Dad, I don't know. But Mom. Mom saves everything. And anyway, nobody, *nobody*, throws away their kid's baby pictures."

"Jake Lucero's great-grandmother brought it from Mexico on a wagon before the Civil War, and it was old then. I hate to think of it ending up as somebody's wine bar."

"Dad."

"Yes." His eyes were still on the armoire.

"Dad."

Finally, he looked at me.

"Ignoring my questions might have worked when I was little. But it doesn't anymore."

He cleared his throat. "Come on. Let's get this piece delivered. Help me." He began to guide the dolly.

"I'm not a little kid, Dad." My voice was level. "Was there a fight in somebody's family? Something embarrassing, or sad?" I waited for him to affirm or deny, but he did neither. "Whatever it was, you can tell me, you know. I'm fourteen."

My father stopped rolling the dolly. He let his arms fall loose at his side. Sweat had appeared on his forehead, and with his silver hair to his shoulders he looked suddenly old. "Please just drop it."

I stepped back. "Oh." I looked around. "So much for a father confiding in his son, I guess."

There was a cobweb on the back of the armoire and I picked my bandanna off my shoulder and snapped at it. I liked the feel and sound of the popping rag. I liked it a lot. I began to walk around the shop, looking for cobwebs.

"So much for a father *trusting* his son." *Pop.*

My father just stood there, watching me.

"Or being *close* to him." *Pop.* "Although, now that I think about it, I'm not sure my father is really very close—" *Pop.* "To *anyone.*" I faced him, considering whether to say what I was thinking. "No wonder

Mom drinks."

His gray eyes blinked. When, after a long minute, he spoke, his voice was quiet and he sounded tired. "I didn't think you knew."

I lowered my voice to match his. "I know." I folded the bandanna and put it into my pocket. "Have known for a very long time."

"It's not much."

I nodded. "I know that, too. Always just little sips." I looked out the window. "But enough little sips that once every three weeks a new bottle shows up behind the china teacups."

Mrs. Johns opened the front door. "Is everything… all right?"

We answered in unison without looking at her. "Fine."

She went back out.

My father sighed and put his eyes back on the armoire. He sighed again. "Let's just get this job done."

"So that's it?" I asked him. "The empty scrapbook, the monogram, Mom's problems…You're not going to talk to me about *any* of it?"

He gazed at the cabinet. "I can't talk to you about any of it."

"Okay." I looked back out the window. "I get it."

We rolled the dolly outside and roped the armoire into our pickup. My dad made sure Mrs. Johns would be home when I got there with the delivery, and then her Suburban pulled out of the potholed lot.

I walked back inside ahead of my dad and went

straight to the drawer under the counter. I took the scrapbook out and pushed the drawer in hard.

"I'll deliver the cabinet." I took the truck keys off the nail. "But after that, well, I don't know. Football... it's, uh, taking a lot of my time."

He just stared at me.

"Tony might work for you," I said, looking away. "He needs the money bad enough to."

"I wish you'd think about this."

I shook my head as I dug into my pocket. I put a dollar bill on the counter and headed for the door. "Sorry," I said, shouldering by him. "I just don't want to work in this junk shop anymore."

Hooks, Lines, and Lures

Floorboards creaked as the boy and his escorts crossed single file through the meeting room toward the stairs at the back of the house. The chalkboard was wiped clean, the wooden lectern vacant, the folding chairs stacked. A militia flag was tacked over the window, lending the room a reddish tint.

The soldiers told the boy to leave his bundled clothes in the kitchen. He tried to fold the flannel shirt, but his hands were shaking too much. He left the clothes in a heap on the counter, next to a tray set with crackers, grape juice, and Dixie cups, and the party started up the stairs.

The boy had been on the second story only a couple of times, once to pick up coloring books for Sunday school and once to deliver a message to an office. At the landing he peered down a hall that was lined with vented doors. Slats were missing from one of the panels, and he glimpsed several computer monitors.

Moving up the narrow stairs, the group climbed to the attic. One by one, the Colonels Williams, the boy, and Private Rossetti ducked under the low doorway and stepped into a spacious, eaved room.

Sunlight streamed through a window. The only furniture was a wooden rocker behind a metal desk and one folding chair. Except for a framed picture of the Reverend General's twin granddaughters, the desktop was clear.

Colonel Shelly squared the folding chair in front of the desk and told the boy, "Please sit." The boy lowered himself stiffly, his back to the door, as creaking sounds began two floors down.

The command of the Soldiers of God's leader echoed up through the hollow walls. "Dismissed." The Reverend General added as he climbed, "Everyone except our guest, that is."

Quietly, the soldiers exited. The boy could hear them on the landing as they addressed their commander in chief in turn, then were excused.

The boy sat still, eyes forward, alert for footsteps behind him. He had heard none when he felt the planks under his chair give, bearing new weight. The boy caught his breath. It seemed odd not to rise and turn and salute, but he had just been ordered to sit and so he didn't move.

"Be at ease," the Reverend General announced from behind the boy. He walked around the desk, carrying a fishing pole in one hand and a tackle box in the other. Rubber waders came to his waist.

Facing the Reverend General, the boy felt an overwhelming urge to salute. He scooted his chair back and began to rise.

With his fishing pole the Reverend General motioned the boy down. "Thank you," he said, "but there's no need to be so formal up here."

The boy sat back, folding his hands in his lap to try to hide the trembling.

"Please excuse me for a minute while I change." The Reverend General left the tackle box on the desk and went into the adjoining room. Through the open door, the boy heard him clip his fishing pole to the wall, shed his waders, and sit on a squeaky bed. The Reverend General called out as he dressed, "I'm sorry to have kept you waiting. But when Colonel Vince paged me that you had been brought in, I had a catch on my line."

When he returned to the room, he was wearing pants held up by suspenders, a work shirt, socks, and slippers. "A big, old, beautiful speckled bass," he continued, his terry cloth shoes flapping as he crossed to the rocker behind the desk. "Could have been twenty inches." The Reverend General showed the length of the fish with his hands. Then he sat down, hooked his thumbs behind the red elastics, and settled into the rocker. "So big and old and beautiful, as a matter of fact," the Reverend General said with a smile, "that I let him go."

The boy didn't smile back. He looked down at the desktop.

The Reverend General began to rock. "Are you comfortable?" he asked.

The boy managed to answer. "Comfortable enough."

"Does your leg hurt?"

"Some."

"I hope Colonel Shelly had a chance to look at it."

"She doesn't think the snake was poisonous."

"Any animal bite can be serious."

"My leg doesn't matter."

"Why not?"

The boy shrugged, eyes still on the desk. "It just doesn't seem very important. Considering, you know, everything."

The Reverend General tipped his chair forward and opened his tackle box. He took out the top tray and began to rifle through the lower portion. The boy could feel the Reverend General looking up at him as he worked. He slipped his hands under his legs to hold them still.

"For heaven's sake," the Reverend General said, "are you nervous?"

The boy didn't answer.

"You've grown up out here at base camp." The Reverend General talked as he sorted the hooks and lures. "We certainly aren't going to hurt you."

The boy lifted his eyes and looked straight at the Reverend General.

Go ahead. Say what you are thinking.

"You killed my mother," the boy said flatly.

The Reverend General dropped the hook he was holding back into the tackle box and shook his head. "I —" He hesitated. "—didn't want to tell you ... before you'd had a chance to rest and eat a meal."

He stood up, and this time the boy's eyes followed him. Leaving his chair rocking, he came around behind the boy and rested his hands lightly on his shoulders. The boy flinched at his touch. The Reverend General asked softly, "How did you know?"

The boy made sure his voice was controlled. "I was hiding, close by, when she was shot."

The Reverend General's fingertips twitched. "I am sorry," he said. "No boy should have to see such a thing."

He walked to the window under the eaves and looked out over base camp. It was a long time before he spoke. "Your father told you war games were scheduled, I suppose?"

"Yes."

The Reverend General nodded. "As part of a training exercise, your father was to play the role of a federal undercover agent escaping with his family. Did he tell you that as well?" He turned to the boy.

The boy knitted his brow. "No...not exactly."

The Reverend General looked back outside. "No live ammunition was to have been used, of course. It was all a very terrible mistake—"

The boy could feel his eyes growing wide. He planted his palms on the desk. "You're saying ..." His body lifted off the chair and his voice rose. "You're saying that my mother's death was an *accident*?"

The Reverend General was still looking out the window. "A very terrible accident."

"But it's not possible—"

The Reverend General's head twisted around. "Why not?" There was a blank look on his face. "What else could you possibly have been thinking?"

Tell him you were thinking it was murder.

"I—"

The Reverend General turned pale. "Surely you don't believe the Soldiers of God shot your mother *on purpose*?"

The boy sat down hard on the seat. His head was spinning.

"It was a training exercise gone bad. A terrible mistake." The Reverend General looked back out the window.

"But, if—" The boy stammered. "If my mother's death was an accident—" He held on to the desk to steady his swaying. He looked around the room. "Then where's my *father*?"

The Reverend General didn't answer.

"My father should be here," the boy persisted. "Right? Shouldn't he? If an accident is what it was."

Still the Reverend General kept his eyes looking out the window.

The boy's voice rose. "Where is my father?"

The Reverend General said nothing. Finally he turned from the window and walked back to his rocking chair, slippers flapping as he crossed the floor. "Actually, we were hoping you could tell us that."

"*What*?"

The Reverend General settled back into the rocker and folded his arms over his stomach. "Yes. It's why we've been so desperately trying to find you both. The two of you need to be here, together, to begin to deal with this tragedy. Unfortunately, however, your father has completely disappeared. His pager isn't working. He may think the exercise is still under way, we don't know. Or maybe he is injured and needs help somewhere out in the woods. All we know is he hasn't come in and we can't find him." The Reverend General looked straight at the boy. "Do you know where he is?"

"You didn't ... shoot him?"

The Reverend General tipped his head to the side. "Shoot him? Why would we shoot him?"

"I thought I heard two shots," the boy said tentatively. "When my mother was killed."

The Reverend General didn't comment. He asked again, "Do you know where he is?"

"You want me to help you hunt down my own father?"

"That's an odd way of putting it. But when you've rested and recovered a bit—truthfully, we were hoping you'd join us for much more than that."

The boy narrowed his eyes. "What do you mean?"

The Reverend General tipped his rocker forward and began to pick through his tackle box. At last he spoke. "You'd be an asset to the movement."

"You're trying ... to recruit me?"

"Well, why not? You've come to Sunday services since you were a little boy. You've learned weaponry at our summer camps. You know—what shall I call it?—our *thinking,* on things."

The boy shook his head in disbelief. He squared his shoulders and folded his hands in front of him on the desk. "Accident or not—why would I join a movement that killed my mother?"

The Reverend General continued to sort. "You mustn't blame the Soldiers of God for your mother's death."

The boy didn't answer.

The Reverend General stopped what he was doing, looked at the boy, and spoke sternly. "Training accidents happen." His voice rose. "There are friendly-fire casualties in every army, even the best. But it's not the army who is to blame, it's the enemy the army fights— in this case, of course, *our* enemy, the American government. The fact that your mother fell here, on our soil, doesn't lessen her sacrifice. She is a victim of the government's excesses, a patriot and a hero as surely as if she had fallen on the battlefield."

The Reverend General sat back in his chair and began to rock again. His face softened. "It is hard for you to see things clearly now. This tragic event is much too fresh in your mind. But we—the Soldiers of God, your friends, your neighbors—we are hoping that after you've had a chance to collect yourself, to begin to grieve and to heal and come to terms with God's sometimes difficult plan, you'll be able to channel your sorrow and anger toward a greater good." He dropped his voice. "I would be proud to have a fine young man like yourself serving by my side."

The boy turned his head and looked out the window. From his chair, all he could see was the sky. "I've never cared much for politics," he said.

"Of course not." The Reverend General continued to rock. "I was fifteen once, too. You care about football and girls and having fun. But fifteen is the brink of manhood. It is a time to begin to turn your mind to more serious pursuits."

The boy put his eyes back on the Reverend General.

"Listen to me." The Reverend General spoke quietly. "You've been raised among us. Your ways are closer to ours than you know. In time, I think you will be *desperate* to join the Soldiers of God, desperate to make sure your mother's death really *counts* for something."

The boy shook his head. "The Soldiers of God blow up buildings with innocent people inside."

The Reverend General's voice became conversational. "Sometimes it is necessary to get people's attention." He shrugged. "Please don't misunderstand me. No one likes civilians to get hurt, but it is an inevitable fact of war. The American government certainly spills plenty of innocent blood when *their* cause is at stake."

The boy hesitated. "I don't think I believe that."

"The government killed mothers and babies at Waco. The Americans defoliated jungles and burned villages in Vietnam. One hundred thousand human beings died in an instant in Hiroshima. Or consider the genocide of the American Indian—painful but necessary, so that white settlement and economic development could begin." The Reverend General gazed at the boy. "Nobody, but nobody, you see, has a monopoly on hurting innocent people."

"I…don't know."

"Of course you don't. Not right now. No one would expect you to be thinking straight after what you've been through. But remember your Bible stories, some of the ones I taught you myself. Didn't the disciple Peter cut off the ear of the soldier who came to arrest Jesus? Didn't Jesus himself turn over the tables in the temple? People might have gotten hurt, probably did." The Reverend General tipped his chair forward and stopped rocking. "You see, you cannot refuse the movement just because the movement is violent. Violence in the name of righteousness is righteous violence."

"I'm sorry. You're confusing me."

The Reverend General slapped the arms of his rocker. "Good." He packed his tackle into the box. "Confusion is a fine first step. We've talked enough for one day." He closed the box and latched it, then stood up and stretched. Putting his thumbs behind his suspenders, he walked around to the boy's side of the desk. "Now, go back to your tent and answer this question."

He doesn't want an answer. Just let him have his say.

The Reverend General bent down close to the boy, so close that the boy could feel his breath on his ear. "Who is going to avenge your mother's death," he whispered, "if you and I don't?"

The boy sat still.

The Reverend General straightened. "So eat a good meal and have a long, hard sleep and plan to stay. Because it's young men like you that our movement is going to depend on someday." He put his thumbs through his suspenders, strolled over to the window, and gazed out over the property. "Now go get some rest," he said offhandedly, his back to the boy.

That much he's right about. You're exhausted, go on.

The boy scooted his chair back and stood up. He turned around to face a framed portrait on the wall beside the door.

He had seen the same print in the Methodist church in town. The subject's light brown hair was clean and brushed. His hazel eyes shone, and his fair skin was tanned and glowing. But there was something different about this particular print. In the corner, on the shoulder of Jesus of Nazareth's muslin robe, someone had painted a militia patch.

The boy waited for the voice in his head to comment, but the voice was quiet.

The Reverend General must have seen the boy studying the portrait because he began to recite scripture.

The boy knew the verse. Matthew 10:34.

"'Do not suppose that I have come to bring peace to the earth. I did not come to bring peace, but a sword.'"

And then the Reverend General added, as the boy walked past the portrait and down the stairs, "He and I are counting on you."

Scraps

A well-regulated militia, being necessary to the security of a free state, the right of the people to keep and bear arms shall not be infringed.

> — Second Amendment to the Constitution of the United States

"The reason the Second Amendment was put into the United States Constitution... (was) so that when officials of the federal and state and local government get out of hand, you can shoot them."

> — Mark Reynolds, member of the Unorganized Militia of Stevens County, Washington, quoted in *False Patriots*, p. 72

"Go up and look legislators in the face, because some day you may have to blow it off."

> — Sam Sherwood, member of the United States Militia Association, quoted in *False Patriots*, p. 73

"[Y]ou can get about four politicians for about 120 foot of rope.... Remember, whenever using it, always try and find a willow tree. The entertainment will last longer."

— Mark Koernke, founder of the Michigan Militia at Large, quoted in *Gathering Storm*, p. 86

"You look at the Old Testament. God did not mind killing a bunch of women and kids. God talks about slaughter. Don't leave one suckling. Don't leave no babies. Don't leave nothing. Kill them! Destroy them."

— Rev. W. N. Otwell, leader of an armed compound in east Texas, quoted in *Gathering Storm*, p. 174

While it is still too soon to say how a new cadre of young leaders will alter the shape of hate in this country, it seems clear that a political and generational change is about to occur.

— from "One Generation Fades... and Another Springs Up," SPLC's *Intelligence Report*, Fall 1999 (issue 96), p. 18

I remember sleet pelting the porch of the diner, outside where a few diehards were still hanging out. It was midnight on December 15 of my sophomore year, and the drizzle in which the Red Cedar high school team had played for the AA state football championship was slowly turning into an ice storm.

Inside the diner, I was splayed on a bench at my usual table with Tony, our running back. Earlier in the night he had crowned me "King of the Bucks" with the wired-together antlers from off the wall. Even the seniors had laughed, so I had let the crown stay on my head for most of the party.

But now the crowd was thinning out. Vince Williams shook my hand, joking about the antlers, and Shelly Williams put her arm around me. The Williamses had closed the Git 'N Go, losing a day of receipts to drive to Tulsa and back for the game. Someone clapped me on the back and I turned around to Sean Taliferro's bear hug.

My parents brought up the rear, my father finger-combing confetti from his shoulder-length hair. My mom kissed Tony and me on the cheek. My dad shook my hand and Tony's, who worked for him now, before leaving arm in arm with my mom. And then, except for the sound of the sleet and occasional laughter from a table of Smithville girls blowing smoke rings, everything was quiet.

Sky swept confetti. Roxanne pulled red and black streamers from the ceiling fan.

Being careful of the antlers, I leaned back against the log wall, closed my eyes, and replayed the day's images. The two scoring long passes to Tony and a quarterback sneak in the freezing mud. The blinking headlights and honking horns out the rear bus window, trailing home down the highway—

"First soph quarterback I ever started."

At the sound of Coach Scotty's voice I opened my eyes. Sky had propped the front door open to cool off the room, and I could hear every word through the screen.

"That kid can sure thread a needle. A' course there's a little crimp in his run, so he ain't the fastest pair of cleats I've coached," Coach Scotty went on. "But that crimp is the reason he performs. Under pressure, his short leg doesn't just force him to throw on the numbers. It forces him to *think*."

Across from me, Tony raised his head off the table. "The rest of us have got to stop making you look so good." He dropped his head again.

I grinned. "He's gonna be embarrassed tomorrow," I said, "when he remembers that he lost control and accidentally complimented somebody."

Stretching my legs out along the bench, I crossed my new sharkskin boots and settled against the wall, arms folded on my chest. The combined odor of fingernail polish and tobacco smoke wafted over from the girls at the Smithville table, and we looked in their direction. Their town was in another school district, but they had driven all the way to Tulsa and back just the same.

"Your fan club," Tony whispered.

One of them, a girl with spiky pink hair and a Smithville cheerleading jacket, finished a fingernail and looked up at me. I could feel my cheeks flush.

"At least I *hope* it's yours," Tony went on. "Too much makeup for me."

I was relieved Tony didn't notice my blushing. I knew he didn't because I would be hearing about it if he had.

Tony stood up and stretched. "Think I'll rotate parties before they get any ideas. There's a senior deal at Bandit's Hollow. Beer and stuff. Wanna come?"

I shook my head and rearranged myself on the bench.

Tony left.

Somebody put money in the jukebox. Willie Nelson…

"Hey."

It was Sky's "Hey" and I opened an eye.

She stood in front of me, eyebrow raised, a basket of chili fries in one hand and two Dr. Pepper bottles in the other. A different song played on the jukebox and the Smithville table was filling its third ashtray.

"Hey," I said back, closing my eye again. "You've

been working too hard, as usual. I hope you're coming to sit with me."

The two of us had gone through a lot of Dr. Peppers and chili fries at this table. Sky set down the food and drinks and scooted onto the bench Tony had vacated. "You're disappointing those girls," she said.

I glanced in their direction. "Why do they keep staring at me?"

Sky's eyes traveled up over my head and I remembered the antlers.

Man. I took the headdress off, set it on the table, and ran my hands through my hair. I leaned over the varnished pine. "How desperate does a person have to be to make a play for a guy wearing antlers?"

She laughed. "When the guy in the antlers is a star quarterback, not very."

I smiled and sat back, studying her. She was only thirteen, but the bib of her work apron was tight in the chest. With her braces off and her hair clipped up for work, she could have passed for sixteen.

"That reporter with the Tulsa paper said as far back as he could check the stats, you're the first sophomore quarterback to take a team to State. Much less to win."

I shrugged and dug into the fries.

"Those college scouts were talking to your parents at the game," she went on.

"They look at lots of kids early."

"Still, it's a big deal."

I smiled at her. "If you say so."

We finished off the fries and Sky went back to

sweeping confetti. I closed my eyes and leaned against the logs, thinking I should have been helping her, but facing the hard truth that in order to do so I would have to move my legs. After a moment I felt my chin dropping and I barely caught myself before I keeled off the bench. Laughter came from the Smithville table and I looked over at them. They waved in my direction and I waved back halfheartedly.

Sky swept under my bench.

"Tony was right," I whispered to her. "I need to get out of here before the attack. Let's go for a walk if you can get off."

"Okay." I was surprised she put down her broom so fast. "Just let me get a sweater." She stuck her head into the kitchen. "Mom, cover for me?"

By the time I had quit yawning and rubbing my eyes, Sky had shed her apron and disappeared into the back of the building. She and her mother had an entire apartment there—living room, two bedrooms plus a spare, bathroom, and a rear-facing porch, everything except a kitchen, which they shared with the diner. Sky left the door open behind her, revealing the apartment's old-fashioned mural-style wallpaper. This front hall was the only part of their home most people ever saw, so it was where Roxanne displayed her daughter's drawings. Roy Roye's place. Bandit's Hollow. The swimming hole. The diner. My mother's garden. Some of the pictures were my favorites and my eyes lingered, until I realized the Smithville girls were watching.

With both hands I lifted one leg off the bench, then the other. The muscles in my thighs hurt, and I could feel bruises to my ribs. I bussed our table, returning the antlers to the wall hook, then took my football poncho off the coat rack and put it on.

Sky reappeared carrying a flashlight. She had changed into blue jeans, a sweater several sizes too big for her, and paint-spattered hiking boots. Now her hair was down.

She talked over the pass-through to her mom. Yes, Sky could walk me home, but she couldn't be gone long. Roxanne would close and wait up.

I said "See ya" to the Smithville girls. To be sure they didn't follow us, I made a point of picking up Sky's hand in front of them. The cheerleader dropped her cigarette when I did it. I smiled to myself and pulled Sky after me onto the porch.

The night air was bracing and instantly cleared my head. The storm had stopped, leaving the roads and wires and trees shining under the colored Christmas lights that decorated the diner year-round.

Sky held up our joined hands and wiggled her fingers. "Uh, do you realize you're holding my hand?"

"Actually"—I looked at her—"I do." Her hand felt so good in mine, I wondered why I had never picked it up before. "Is it ... okay?"

She thought a moment, then looked out at the shimmering night. "More than okay," she said, and squeezed my fingers as we headed out into the ice-glazed town.

Night into Day

On his way back down the attic stairs, the boy was met by Private Rossetti. The soldier still carried a rifle, but this time he led the boy instead of pointing the weapon at his back.

In the kitchen, the Colonels Williams stood waiting. The boy told them he had been excused and asked if they would mind, please, letting him use the bathroom.

Colonel Shelly went upstairs to receive orders from the Reverend General as Private Rossetti escorted the boy to the bathroom and waited outside. The boy drank his fill of rusty water from the faucet and splashed his face. When he came out, Private Rossetti handed his clothes back to him. He walked the boy out of the farmhouse, across the assembly yard, and into an army tent staked at the treeline.

The moment they were inside the flap, Private Rossetti put down his gun. The two of them stood for a moment, looking at each other.

Until today, the boy hadn't seen his friend since the night of the championship game four months before.

Tony had been busted for smoking dope at Bandit's Hollow that night, and as a result, had been kicked off the football team. The next day Tony hadn't shown up at school. When the boy had gone looking for him, Tony's grandfather said Tony had left town to take a job in McCurtain County.

"I thought you were cutting down trees for Weyerhaeuser," the boy said.

"I was," Private Rossetti answered. "But now I'm not."

The boy sat on the edge of the cot.

Private Rossetti stayed on his feet. "I've been a little on the spot here," he said. "Us being friends and me being new and all." He coughed. "Colonel Shelly dressed me down for being so rough on you out in the yard. Guess I was trying to prove myself, or something. Which I shouldn't have been."

"Well. You've got a job to do."

"Yeah." Private Rossetti coughed again. "I do." He took his place on the camp stool and rested the M-16 across his knees.

The boy spread his damp clothes at the foot of the cot, lay down, and stared up at the tenting. He tried to think back over his conversation with the Reverend General in the farmhouse, but his brain felt numb.

The canvas over his head turned dusky in the fading light, and the sound of spoons clicking against aluminum camp plates drifted in. Sergeant Roye ducked through the flap and gave food to the boy and to Private Rossetti. The boy lifted the pie pan off the top of his plate. Steam curled from creamed chipped beef on white bread and boiled butter beans. He sat up and began to eat.

Colonel Shelly stuck her head in. "Are you needin' anything?"

The boy could have devoured another plateful of food, but he didn't ask for more. Instead, he told her about the ticks in his hair and the blister on his heel.

Colonel Shelly disappeared, then returned with first aid. She killed the ticks with mineral oil and tweezed them out of his scalp. She gave him antiseptic and a Band-Aid for his foot, and a clean pair of thick, dry socks.

When she had left, the boy pulled up a blanket and lay back and rubbed his stomach. With his belly full, it seemed easier to concentrate.

Could his mother's killing have somehow been an accident? He tried to remember exactly what he had seen and heard from the log.

Were the soldiers who came for your mother upset at what they found?

One of them was throwing up, I think.

But that could be a natural reaction to seeing a dead body.

Yes.

Other than that, did the soldiers seem troubled?

No, not really. Not at all.

Did any of them say anything about a mistake or an accident?

One said it was "sorrowful duty."

And they were ready with a body bag, weren't they?

So where did the bag come from if they weren't expecting to use it?

Right. And didn't it sound like a sniper rifle that took her down?

Uh-huh. How could a sniper not know he's got live ammunition in his gun? I don't think a person can even load any other kind of ammunition into a sniper rifle, do you?

No, I don't.

Whoever it was, they knew they weren't firing blanks or paint balls.

Not to mention ... one more thing. What about your dog?

Pet! Somebody killed Pet.

You're sure, I suppose. Pet couldn't have just gotten hurt when she jumped, could she?

I heard automatic gunfire. She never even raised her head.

So why, when you were in the farmhouse, didn't you point out all these discrepancies?

I don't know. I really don't. I was half in shock, and tired and scared, I guess. I've been trying so hard *not* to think about what I saw, it's hard to remember everything, now that I need to. And there's something about the Reverend General. When you're in front of him, he can sound so... reasonable.

You mean, while he's lying.

Yeah. Which is the scariest thing yet.

I agree.

One good thing, though. I think my father is still alive.

Why do you say that?

Because the Reverend General was trying to get me to help look for him. To, you know, give something away about where he might be.

Or it could just be another lie. If your father is dead, or caught, the Soldiers of God certainly aren't going to tell you that.

True. See what I mean, my thinking's all foggy. I can't tell the tricks from the truth anymore. I've been too close to them for too long. So long that I don't know the answer to the Reverend General's question. So long that if I stay here, in time, I'm afraid—in spite of my mother's death, in spite of everything—I'll join. Or if I somehow manage to keep my wits and *don't* ... well ...

The Soldiers of God aren't going to let you walk away.

I know too much. I'm either going to end up dead, or one of them.

You have to get out.

Now.

Use what they have taught you.

The boy remembered the rules of terrorist engagement. Attack at the weakest point. Divert attention from the main operation. Keep the logistics simple.

He thought back to his circle of captors. What was the weakest point? A point weak enough for a fifteen-year-old boy to break through? Would one of the soldiers help him?

Go around the circle.

Taliferro. Martindale. Redhawk. Johns. Murry.

Murry. Coach. Lucero. Lucero. Roye. Wolfman.
Wolfman's friend. Back to Taliferro.

You're forgetting.

Williams. Williams. Rossetti. The Reverend General.

But some of the ones he knew the best were the
most committed soldiers. And none would disobey
orders.

Go around again.

The boy went around the circle one more time.
When he got to ten o'clock, his eyes popped open. The
weakest point wasn't a person. The boy almost sat up,
but then he remembered where he was and he didn't.

He pictured Wolfman, smoking in front of the
round barn. Wolfman should be careful with that cigarette—that old round barn would go up like a Roman
candle. And if it did, if the entire stockpile of ammunition and explosives blew, one boy escaping in the
woods would be the least of the soldiers' concerns.

The boy didn't know a lot about fuses and detona-
tors. But maybe he didn't have to.

He lifted his head and looked toward the camp stool.
Private Rossetti cracked his gum, staring into space, his
gun across his knees. The boy slid his fingers into his
shirt pocket, feeling for the Lucky Strikes. Being careful
not to rattle the cellophane, he slipped the matchbook
out, opened it under the blanket, and counted the
matches between his fingers.

Three matches. Two cigarettes. And one decrepit,
highly ignitable round barn.

—

By now the dark was so intense that the fabric over the boy's head wasn't any color at all. It was as if the tent had melted away, clearing his view. Low voices were talking outside when a soldier lifted the flap and looked in.

"Come on," the soldier whispered to Private Rossetti. It could have been Wolfman. "Your quarterback ain't goin' nowhere."

Private Rossetti cracked his gum but didn't move.

"Don't be so uptight," the soldier went on. "The Rev's holed up in meetings and we'll be right here."

Still, Private Rossetti didn't stir.

"I got us some dope."

Private Rossetti's knees popped as he stood, then leaned over the boy's cot. He pulled the blanket back from the boy's face. His breath was warm. The gum was spearmint. And then he left.

The boy could hear them on the other side of the tent. Again a soldier lifted the flap. "Aw, he's sick," somebody said. "And asleep." This time the boy thought it was the other guy in the Pontiac. Outside, somebody flicked a lighter, and the soldier lowered the tarp.

The aroma of marijuana seeped through the canvas. The Soldiers of God didn't care about drugs being illegal, but they could get in serious trouble for smoking dope on duty. A little dope-smoking was an excellent development, the boy thought. It wouldn't hurt his chances if his guards got stoned.

Go if you're going and do it now.

The boy stuffed his extra clothes under the blankets, except for his belt, which he buckled around his hips, over the camos he was still wearing. He eased his weight to the ground at the back of the tent and flattened his backbone against the earth. The canvas was rigid, but the boy squeezed under, immediately rolling to his hands and knees and crawling behind a tree. He stood and began to circle, slinking between the pines and checking constantly behind him.

Three figures squatted in front of his tent. Across camp, a purple light zapped mosquitoes. There was no sign of the Pontiac; near where it had been parked, a campfire had burned to coals. A couple of soldiers sat around the firepit in lawn chairs. Someone had strung a line between the dinner bell and the farmhouse porch, and laundry hung drying. At headquarters, all the lights were on, including on the third floor.

The boy made it to his first substantial cover, a huge woodpile, and crept behind the stacked cords of quartered logs. There was a toolshed behind the logs where axes and saws and hatchets were kept for chopping wood. A hatchet would be too loud for the job ahead of him, but it could be useful in his next trek. On his way back he would steal one.

A six-foot open stretch loomed between the woodpile and the round barn. The boy held his breath and walked across.

A chain clinked as Old Sal, the militia's Doberman, picked her head up off her paws. The boy was surprised to see her here—usually she bedded down in the farmhouse.

Remember, she knows you.

He held out his hand for the dog to sniff, then rubbed behind her ears. Old Sal lowered her head and went back to sleep.

The boy found a spot on the far side of the barn where the siding was popping loose, and he pried the board off a bit more. The wood creaked; he held his breath. He unthreaded his rope belt and wrapped it around the boards. Fraying the ends, he draped the strings down the slats.

He dug the Lucky Strikes out of his pocket, put a cigarette in his mouth, and took out the matches. He drew one across the striking surface. It was loud, and the flame didn't catch. He slipped the match into his pocket and drew the second match across. It struck, and he lit the cigarette.

Holding the glowing tip to the frayed ends of the rope fibers, the boy leaned against the barn and puffed. The wood felt soft against his forehead. He could hear the wind bumping branches against the structure, and he sheltered the fuse with his body to block any gusts. He puffed harder, and the twirl of strings caught and began to burn. He moved the tip of the cigarette to the next strand.

Shouts. Time was up.

The dinner bell began to clang, announcing emergency orders, the signal to come in and form up. There was yelling and tramping and cocking of weapons and Old Sal was alert on her chain.

The boy peeked from the far side of the barn. On the opposite side of camp, flashlight beams danced across tents and laundry as the bell continued to clang. He dropped the butt inside the barn for good measure, and put the remaining one match and one cigarette in his pocket. He checked the fuse. It was burning well and the slats were catching. And then he walked away.

Directions were not a problem here, even in the dark. The boy had been coming to base camp since he was five years old and he knew exactly where he was.

This time he headed south. He would follow the abandoned railroad track to Octavia. That little town was even closer to base camp than Red Cedar, and a bus came through on 259 twice a day. He'd go to Broken Bow or Idabel—they were big enough to be fairly safe—and call the diner from there.

He was thirty paces away before he remembered the hatchet, twenty paces farther away before he remembered Old Sal. He should have unstaked her so she wouldn't get hurt in the blast. But he couldn't go back now.

The boy walked faster, although he didn't need to, because soon the explosion would make one missing boy a very low priority. His leg hardly hurt, his shoulder was better, and his heart was full in his chest. Who'd have ever guessed a fifteen-year-old kid could pull off a stunt like blowing up the stockpile of the Soldiers of God?

He smiled, estimating how long it would take the

fire to catch the building. He had lit the fuse maybe two minutes ago. The wood had been very rotten, and the strong wind would help. Flames would kick up fast.

The boy looked up at the still pine needles. What had happened to the wind? Branches had been blowing against the barn. He had never known a night wind to die down so fast.

He thought back. Low voices and the click of a cigarette lighter. The aroma of marijuana seeping in. The distinct zap of a mosquito light. A fire burned to coals, not flames. And when he had turned his back on camp, the laundry under the dancing flashlights was still hanging limp on the line.

The boy stopped walking, closed his eyes, and prayed for a breeze to blow across his face. None did.

Branches had not been bumping against the barn.

He tried to think of other possibilities, but there were no good ones. Mice or bats or raccoons wouldn't have made such insistent knocking noises. Wind blowing something against the structure was the only explanation he could think of. Except for someone tapping. Someone who had heard a person prying a board or lighting a match.

Could the tapping have had a pattern? Could it have been Morse code? S.O.S.? He didn't know.

But he knew that even the faintest sounds, when tapped against the wall of a round barn, could be heard clearly from anyplace on the circle. He also knew he could be wrong, prayed that he was, but how could he take that chance?

The boy was running back, had been running back, long enough for sweat to break out under his arms and on his chest. Except that it wasn't very far, so the sweat must have been from fear.

The boy ran hard. He ran blind. He scratched his face raw on the pine needles and the sharp, whipping branches, and already he was behind the woodpile.

The Soldiers of God were on the far side of camp and Colonel Vince was calling search-order sectors through a megaphone. The boy needed another diversion.

Squatting behind the logs, he dug the third match out of his pocket and struck it fast and firm. The flame rose on the first try.

He burrowed down through the wood chips to layers that were years old. Cupping his hands over a nest of splinters, he blew. The flame caught, and he spread it down the line of leaves that had drifted against the back of the woodpile.

Then he stepped into the shed and took the first axe he felt off a nail in the wall. He walked fast past the gap, pulled up Old Sal's stake, and ran to his handmade fuse.

The fire had burned halfway up the rope, and the slats were flaming briskly. He could possibly chop the fire out, but if he did, there would never be time to start it again. If the boy's father was inside, the two of them were going to need that explosion to have any chance of getting away from a camp full of soldiers, already up and armed.

On the other side of the barn, loud pops and crackles came from the direction of the woodpile and the night sky began to glow. Old Sal barked wildly and now there was running and shouting.

The boy unsnapped the leather guard from the axe blade. He picked a place close to the hole, keeping his eye on the flames. This time the chaos would cover the noise.

He slammed the axe into the barn and pulled it free. Two, three, four times the boy swung at the rotting wood. He ripped the splintered planks off with his hands and climbed through.

There was more smoke inside than out. He covered his mouth and pinched his nose and bent low to the ground. Only soldiers were allowed in the barn and the boy didn't know his way. There was an aisle around the perimeter. One hand to the splintery wall, he crept along it. A flashlight had been left on top of one of the wooden crates. He picked it up and turned it on.

Boxes stamped "Dynamite." Bags with "Ammonium Nitrate" printed on them. Drums of gasoline. The heat would ignite the chemicals long before the flames reached them. Cases of ammo clips. A pyramid of hardshell gun cases. And then the boy stopped. On the dirt path, bound and gagged and leaning back against the wall, was his father.

David Morgan lifted his chin to the light, squinting to see who had come. His eyelids were bruised and swollen.

The boy didn't stop to gaze back into the bruised eyes, or to take out the gag, or to say one word. With the axe blade, he sawed at the knot around his father's ankles. After what seemed like forever it cut through.

The boy untangled the rope and lifted his father to his feet, hands still bound. He put one arm around his father and carried the axe in the other.

His father's legs buckled and the boy tried to take the weight. "Hurry," was all the boy said, once, under his breath, as much to himself as to his dad.

After what seemed like many times longer than the flames should have needed to reach the explosives, the boy and his father reached the splintery hole he had chopped. David Morgan somersaulted through and landed with a thud. The boy dropped the flashlight and axe after him, then ducked and tumbled through himself, landing hard on his hurt shoulder.

Father and son were rolling away, together, when the exploding barn turned night into day...

Scraps

Now we are engaged in a great civil war, testing whether that nation, or any nation so conceived and so dedicated, can long endure.

—from Abraham Lincoln's Gettysburg Address, Nov. 19, 1863

Voices in a Room

Shielding himself from the rain of shingles and nails, the boy covered his head with his arms and curled on the rag rug in a spare room that wasn't spare anymore. Ears ringing and eyes shut against the blast, he waited for the smoke and chemical fumes to clear from his head. Odd that his ears were ringing; usually they never did. Oh, this ringing was intermittent. It must be a telephone.

Footsteps. And then the ringing stopped, answered in another room.

The silence felt peaceful. The boy's muscles relaxed and he lifted his eyes to the wallpaper.

The pattern was old-fashioned, a faded woodland mural, stamped and re-stamped all around him. In the corner of the scene, a raccoon nibbled. A southern yellow pine anchored the edge of the picture and spread its branches over. Oak leaves and acorns trimmed the foreground, foliage sure to hide ticks. The middle ground was cut by a swift river where a generic species of snake sunned on a rock. Across the water, the red dot of a hunter's cap disclosed its owner, stalking among the trees. The hunter had pitched his camp in the distance. Firepit, tent, and a makeshift laundry line were tucked under the pines. And then the mural repeated in every direction.

The boy closed his eyes, resting. It took effort to stay out here on the surface of things.

Again the phone was ringing, and the boy's eyes popped back open. People might be coming. They came sometimes, after this much calling. The boy had kept careful track of the cycles of light and dark on the other side of the drawn curtains, and he knew that twelve days had passed since he had been in this room, twelve days during which people—strangers, always—had been calling and coming.

Fully alert now, he listened. Car doors shutting. Footsteps tramping across the porch. These people had phoned from the parking lot if they were here already. Knocking. The diner must be closed or they would have walked right in.

The screen door stretched open on its coil and the voices and footsteps moved inside. The group split. Some stayed in the restaurant and some came into the living room, on the other side of the boy's door.

The boy uncurled his body and brushed the shingles and nails from his clothes. He crept to the door, moving slowly to keep the floorboards from creaking, and put his eye to the keyhole.

Uniforms. Navy-blue windbreakers with big block letters that said "FBI." Some of the people took off their jackets, revealing shirtsleeves. Some wore ties.

All wore leather shoes.

Dressed in a T-shirt and jeans, Sky sat on the edge of the couch, looking pale but composed.

A woman reached into a hard-shell case and took out a legal pad and pen. A man tapped a microphone, then set up a machine and put his hands on the keys. "Let's get this down," the woman said, and the man at the machine began to press the silent keys.

The woman spoke formally about her prior interviews with Sky, expressing her appreciation for Sky's cooperation. "Thank you," she concluded, "for your willingness to have your sworn statement taken today, ensuring that your testimony will be preserved while events are fresh in your memory."

Sky nodded. She sat straight-backed, her hands in her lap. It reminded the boy of the way he had sat in front of the Reverend General in the farmhouse, except that her hands weren't shaking.

"Please swear the witness," the woman directed, and the man told Sky to raise her right hand.

The boy took his eye away from the keyhole. Where was Roxanne? She should be here, to help her daughter through this. But then he remembered the voices and footsteps in the front part of the building. Separate interviews would be one of this army's rules of interrogation.

He put his eye back as the woman was finishing. "And so we'll begin with you simply telling what you remember. Is that all right?"

Sky nodded and tucked her hair behind her ears.

"Are you comfortable?"

She nodded again.

"You have to answer out loud, Sky." The woman pointed to the man pressing the keys. "So the court reporter can make a record."

Sky nodded again. "I mean, okay."

"Fine. Why don't you start with the morning of the ambush."

"Okay. Well. Like I told you before, first I knew anything was wrong, was that morning."

Someone reached in and handed her a glass of water. She took a drink and gave the glass back.

"I was sorting silverware when my mom came in running. She said Blanche Morgan had been shot out in the hills and that the Reverend General was going crazy over at base camp, threatening to hang his own people if somebody didn't find Mrs. Morgan's husband and son and bring them in." She exhaled shakily.

"You're doing fine, Sky," the woman said.

Sky nodded. The color was coming back to her cheeks.

"Remember to breathe," the woman went on, "and keep going just like you are. I'll stop you if I need to clarify anything."

"Okay." Sky's hair was still behind her ears, but she tucked it back again anyway. "I went out on the porch, our porch, here, at the diner, and looked up the road. I could see the Soldiers of God already at the Morgans' place, and some other people standing around, so I ran up there, too. The soldiers had gotten the Morgans' pajamas to scent the hounds, and a lot of townies—"

"Townies?"

"People, you know, who aren't necessarily militia. People like me and my mom."

The woman nodded and Sky kept going. "The townies, everybody really, they were all, like, afraid, and nervous and excited and everything, and they followed the soldiers out to the hills."

"Excuse me, Sky. But wasn't it dangerous, following the soldiers out to the hills?"

"Yeah, I guess it was. I mean, sure, the Soldiers of God didn't want people out there, walking around in the middle of their hunt. But I guess there wasn't much they could do."

Someone poured more water. This time when Sky took the glass she smiled and said, "Thank you." She scooted back and propped her arm on a cushion as she sipped the drink.

"What happened next?"

"The hounds—the soldiers got hounds from Cherry Martindale, she keeps dogs and trains them and stuff—and those hounds, ma'am, those hounds went straight to the Morgans' son. I know because I was out there by then. Most everybody in Red Cedar was out there by then, when those dogs started goin' crazy around that old log."

The boy stood up straight. Around that old log? Around that old log? What was she saying? He put his ear back.

"The soldiers took an axe and busted him outta that

old hollow tree."

The boy's stomach began to cramp, but this time he didn't take his ear away. He had never even gotten out of the log?

"And with us all standing around gawking, well, they couldn't really hurt him, not right there in front of everybody."

The boy began to shiver. He wrapped his arms around himself and stiffened his jaw to keep his teeth from chattering.

"He was sick, that much you could see—white, and cold to the touch. Me and my mom, we said we'd take him to the hospital, which was when somebody drove up in the Morgans' truck. Said they'd found the truck, and the Morgans' dog, shot dead, out on the road to the base camp. Said the truck was just abandoned out there, keys and all. Well, he was still not walkin' or talkin' or even moving much, so we stretched him out in the truck bed, and I wrapped him up with a rug from one of the crates that had tipped over back there. And then my mom got in the front and drove—"

The boy stepped away from the door. He dropped his head back and looked up at the ceiling.

He hadn't even walked. In his mind he had walked. Walked away, far away, on his own, even with one leg short by half an inch. He had guessed some time ago that he hadn't really saved his dad and exploded the round barn. That part was too much, a fairy tale. But he thought that he had at least made it here, to the diner, on his two legs.

It would be the easiest thing, the boy thought as he began to stir, to just not return—to consciousness, or Red Cedar, or the nightmare of the Soldiers of God. Stay in the log and go back to sleep and forget it all ...

It was what he had done.

The boy sank to his knees. Shoulders slumped, eyes closed, he stayed that way for a long time.

When, finally, he stepped back to the keyhole, Sky had folded her legs sideways under her and the water glass was empty.

"After he started coming out of his shock, he could remember things pretty well up to the time he crawled into the log. Then he would just shut down. The doctors thought he could've suffered a trauma-induced memory loss, like maybe he'd seen something he shouldn't have. They said he might not ever get that memory back. Or that his mind might just make something up to fill in the gap. They told us what he needed most was rest and they let us bring him here.

"Which is pretty much the end of what there is to tell. Because by suppertime, helicopters and SWAT teams and FBI and ATF were swarmin' all over these parts, which you know about. Thing is, that bust practically turned Red Cedar into a ghost town. Everyone who wasn't arrested ran outta here and now there's just a few families left. Hardly enough to keep the diner open, much less make any money at it."

Enough.

The boy crawled to the rug. He found the piece from his mother's yellow flowered skirt, lay down, and put his cheek to the fabric. He stretched his right arm up the inside of the log and locked his gaze on the forest, but the story didn't start.

His heart thumped. Had he stayed out here so long that he couldn't slip back between the trees? He began to pant.

The story will start if you need it to.

Thank goodness you are here.

I am always here. Go ahead and start the story if you want to. I think the story is going to be irrelevant very shortly, anyway.

You do?

So much activity, just to take one girl's sworn statement? Something else must be happening. But for now, just start the story. And remember, even if you don't hear me again, I am always with you.

It sounded too much like a goodbye. "Wait!" he shouted. "Don't go!"

On the other side of the door, the talking stopped.

Quick, the boy had to start the story. The voice had said to, which was right, because the voice was in the story. The two of them could talk there.

Cold. Inside the log, the boy shivered himself awake. The rubbery smell was gone.

In the living room, a cell phone began to beep.

Damn it. The boy got up, walked to the door, and kicked the knotty pine with his boot as hard as he could. He yelled, "Don't you people know I can't think straight with all this going on!"

Silence. And then, as the boy stood listening,

sounds began again, outside. More car doors and footfalls on the steps.

It was too much. He hurried back to the rug.

The screen door stretched open and banged shut, and one set of footsteps strode through the building, toward the spare room that wasn't spare anymore.

The boy felt his eyes open wide. He'd had visitors before. Doctors and lawyers and investigators, mostly, he thought. Always, they asked what he remembered. The boy remembered things, just not the kinds of things they wanted him to. But no visitor, ever, had just barged into his room.

The footsteps stopped at his door.

Frantically, the boy searched the forest for a place to hide. High in the corner, one section of the wallpaper had popped loose and was beginning to curl away from the wall. Odd that he hadn't noticed before. He moved his eyes to another section and fixed his gaze.

The crystal knob twisted and the door swung open and this time it wasn't a stranger. The story skidded into being.

Cold. Inside the log, the boy shivered himself awake. The rubbery smell was gone.

But the boy was only hearing the words, not living them, and his father was standing in the doorway.

The boy rocked, unbreathing, his cheek against the yellow fabric, his eyes fixed on the man in front of him.

His father dropped to his knees. "Walker." His eyes were gray but they didn't glow. There were creases in his face. Sky and Roxanne stood behind him and many more figures hovered in the shadows, a silent army in shirtsleeves.

Wait. Go back. What he said, that was it.

But the boy didn't need to go back. He had heard. He was hearing everything now.

His father, still kneeling, said it again. "Walker."

The boy had seen the word "WALKER." The word was tooled into his leather belt. But the boy thought it was what he did, not who he was. Walker: one who walked; one who moved forward by standing erect and placing one foot in front of the other even if one leg was short by half an inch; one whose boots had worn a path into the planks of a spare room that wasn't spare anymore; a boy who walked out of the woods to meet his father at the diner.

Walker stood up. He didn't crawl out of the log and brush himself off. There was no log.

He turned his eyes away from his father and walked slowly around the room, taking all of it in for the first time. His heel felt fine inside the boot, no blister there. He didn't look for a puncture wound in his thigh. His shoulder seemed okay.

There was a rocker, a window, and a metal desk with a folding chair. An electric clock sat on the desk, its cord dangling, unplugged. A narrow bed was made up with fresh, turned-down linens. There was cross-stitching along the hem of the pillowcase.

In the corner, crates were stacked on the floor. They were the same crates that had once been in the back of his family's pickup, except now they were empty. The boy walked the perimeter of the room again, looking harder. This time he found a bookcase.

He ran his hand along the top shelf. There was a collection of books and he touched each worn binding. The book of fairy tales his mother used to read to him on the porch swing. His field guides and survival manuals. He slipped out a gilt-edged volume, and it fell open to a dog-eared page.

Keats, he knew the poem well. He had heard Roy Roye struggle to read it many times.

I had a dove and the sweet dove died;
And I have thought it died of grieving:
O, what could it grieve for? Its feet were tied,
With a silken thread of my own hand's weaving.

The sweetness stored back in the honeycomb of the boy's brain began to leak from its sealed-off cell. The boy wiped a tear off the page, closed the book, and put it back.

Next came his father's militia books, then a Bible, and last an old leather scrapbook. Objects were so magically appearing under the boy's fingertips, he hesitated, wondering. If he opened the scrapbook, would the little black corners be filled with pictures and mementos? The book was thin and he didn't think so. He went on to the next shelf.

His father's dartboard, with no darts. A coloring-book page with "To Mom" in a child's handwriting under the picture. Two Dr. Pepper bottles. Pet's old leash and an arm cast signed by Tony Rossetti. The boy's eyes stopped on a propped drawing. The proportions weren't perfect, but there was something about the sketch that exactly captured the feeling of getting set, hunkering back, and cocking an arm to whip the ball on its arc.

There was an empty .308 Winchester bullet box. Copies of the *Daily Oklahoman* and the *Tulsa World* were stacked. The boy recognized the editions. They carried stories about a championship game and a surprising sophomore quarterback. The boy's football was propped beside the newspapers and he reached to pick it up, but then he saw what was on the bottom shelf and he didn't.

Walker got down on his knees. He lifted the rosewood china chest with both hands and set it on the floor.

He wiped his cheek with his flannel cuff, then put his hands over his face and bowed his head. He remembered the sharp angle at which the truck bed had pitched, sliding the chest out from under the tarp. Please, he prayed, don't let another piece of her be broken.

Then he unlatched and opened the lid. The tea service was packed in pine shavings. There was a teapot, a sugar bowl, a cream pitcher, and a set of cups and saucers. He lifted each dish out and set it on the shelf. No chips or cracks that he could see. Holding the last teacup, he ran his finger over the monogram. The china was cold to his touch.

Walker's father had come into the room and was kneeling beside him. "When we moved here," his father said, "we weren't supposed to bring anything that could identify us. But I couldn't make your mother leave the tea set behind. It was a wedding gift from her grandmother. The two of them used to play with the dishes—" His voice broke but he managed to finish. "—when your mother was a little girl."

Walker asked flatly, "What does 'L,E,F' stand for?"

His father reached into the chest and searched through the shavings. He found a small envelope, blew the pine dust from it, and slipped out a gold-trimmed card. The penmanship was full of flourishes.

Use the teacups, chérie. They are less delicate than you think.—Grandmère LeFrançois

"LeFrançois is your mother's maiden name," his father explained. "The dishes were shipped from France to your mother's family in Louisiana a hundred years before the Civil—"

Walker turned and held up his palm. "Not now," he said.

His father nodded and looked back at the teacup. Then, nesting his hands, he reached out to his son.

For a long moment, Walker didn't move. When he finally set the teacup inside his father's fingers, his father brought it to his cheek. He held the cup against his face, eyes closed, as if he were breathing in the china's scent. Then he passed the cup back.

Walker lifted the teacup to his own face. Was there a fragrance of rainwater and honeysuckle and his mother's garden? No, only pine shavings and porcelain.

He packed the china away, latched the rosewood chest, and set it on the shelf. Then he looked over his shoulder at Sky, who had taken his father's place in the doorway.

Walker went to her. He wrapped his arms around her waist and leaned his head on her shoulder and held on. Everyone except the boy's father stepped back into the shadows of the living room.

After a while, Walker's father stood up. "I am here for you when you need me," he said. Then he left.

Walker let go of Sky. "Wait."

His father turned on his heel and came back to the doorway.

Walker straightened and dropped his arms to his side. "I needed you twelve days ago. Where were you then?"

His father hesitated a moment, then spoke slowly. "After I left you in the log, I came to the diner and filed my report. Washington ordered me in. My superiors said it was too dangerous to stay in town without my cover. I was needed to help plan the raid, and they picked me up and kept me away." He cleared his throat. "Of course I argued with the orders. I said I wouldn't leave without you. I told them my son's life was at stake." He cleared his throat again. "They said,

'More lives than your son's are at stake.'"

Walker studied his father. "Did you save those lives?"

His father looked away, then back. "We never know for sure about the lives we save," he said. "We only know for sure about the lives we lose."

"That's not a good enough answer," Walker said.

"I know."

The curtains were open and morning was finally beginning to brighten the room. Walker sat in the folding chair at the desk, working under the lamp Sky had brought to him. Scraps of torn paper lay where they had fallen. A bottle of rubber cement was open. A tray of food sat untouched.

Sky was asleep in the rocker and Walker's father snored on a pallet outside the door. All the other visitors had gone.

Walker folded the crease in the paper forward and back, forward and back. With patience and practice, it was amazing how easily the wood fibers came apart in his hands.

His scrapbook had to be fat. Of course he would have to tear up a great deal in order to accomplish that. He had already started ripping up his father's militia books and articles, pasting in and labeling the quotations. The militia movement wasn't the chronological beginning of the boy's journey, but it was the origin of everything he could remember, and so it was a good place for his scrapbook to start.

Next would come Sky's drawing and the sports articles, personal things like that. It was hard to imagine ripping his mother's favorite poems from their gilt-edged book, Walker thought as he creased, but he was strong enough to do it.

Last would come documents that his parents had entrusted to the government for storage more than a decade ago. Earlier that night, when his father had finally understood what it was Walker wanted to do, he had phoned Washington. Walker had heard the conversation from his room.

"After all this family has given," his father had said, his voice rising, "and assuming the prosecution wants a cooperating witness on the stand, those boxes better be in Red Cedar tomorrow."

Walker had no doubt, the boxes would arrive the next day—today, now. His father was good at getting things like that done, and there was no reason to keep the documents classified now that the Red Cedar operation was over.

Wedding portraits and family trees and birth announcements and obituaries and old letters and journals and even his own baby pictures had been promised, although Walker had lost interest in the specifics. Still, it would be good to have the papers here. They would make his book fat. First in time, last in his book, because until now he had lived his life without any of it.

Sky stirred and Walker looked over at her, asleep in her blue jeans, bare feet tucked into the chair. Behind the rocker, up high in the corner, the loose section of wallpaper had been stripped away. Walker had pulled the mural down in the middle of night and now it covered the endpapers in his scrapbook. He didn't like seeing the hardened, yellowed paste the stripping had exposed, and he looked back at Sky.

She stirred again, and Walker clicked off the lamp and closed the drapes. He tiptoed to the bed, threw back the linens, and dragged a blanket off. He went to the rocker and spread the cover over her.

Sky spoke drowsily without opening her eyes. "Someday you'll have to forgive him."

"Why?" Walker asked, as he tucked the blanket in around her.

"Because one parent is barely enough."

She turned and went back to sleep, and Walker went back to his tearing.

Twilight,
Four Months Later

The floorboards creaked as Walker rocked in the chair, breathing in the scent of the pines coming through the open window. He had moved the rocker to the opposite corner of the room so he could study the wall where he had ripped down the paper so many nights before. Spring and most of summer had gone by since then, and it no longer bothered him to look at the hardened paste. He understood now what he hadn't then. A scar was a sign of healing.

His eyes roamed over the rest of the room, almost as bare as when he hadn't seen it at all. The mattress was stripped down to the ticking. The crates and china chest were packed and ready for loading, and the rag rug was rolled and tied. A broom and dustpan were propped in the corner.

The room was going to be spare again because Walker was leaving with his father. The first stop would be Louisiana, and then they would head east, to a little town where his father's parents were buried under a headstone that didn't say "Morgan."

Of course there would be trips back to LeFlore

County. Walker and his father would be traveling regularly between Washington and Oklahoma as long as what the media had dubbed the Red Cedar Trials were pending. But Walker didn't think he would ever live in this town again.

Which was about as much as he could say about what would happen next, he thought as he rocked. His future lay before him like the forest in the night. Now and then lights flickered over the trunks of the trees, so he knew the forest was out there. But ghostly, fleeting glimpses of what lay ahead were the most he ever got.

Walker listened to the familiar sounds drifting in through his open door. Dishes and silverware clinked. Sky and her mother and two new employees called orders back and forth.

Red Cedar still had a vacant feeling—he knew because he and Sky walked during the slow part of the afternoon—but in the past few months the diner had become a tourist and media destination. He smiled at the thought of Roxanne, who had started pricing Sky's art and hanging it out front in the restaurant.

Walker rocked a long time, until the supper noises and twilight had completely faded away and the clock said eight-fifty. His father would be here soon, right on time, he knew. He stood up and went to the thick scrapbook on the desk. He turned on the lamp and flipped through the pages.

The book ended with articles from newspapers and magazines his father had sent, now cut with scissors. The stories described "law enforcement's raid on the tiny town of Red Cedar," and the "instrumental testimony of an undercover agent placed by the FBI." They reported indictments for "possession of and trafficking in illegal weapons and explosives, and conspiracy to destroy government property and overturn the United States government."

Walker ran his eyes over the final article in his book, concerning a statement issued by the Attorney General not long after the storming of the base camp. "The Department of Justice is gratified by the arrests of the leaders of the Red Cedar cell; however, in the wake of the raid, co-conspirators are believed to have dispersed and remain at large. The militia movement's goals remain unshaken. Those goals include escalating violence against the federal government and its citizens."

It was true, he thought. The Soldiers of God had never laid a hand on him, but he was a victim of their violence.

Walker touched the words he had torn from the Bible and glued, like a caption, over the woodland wallpaper scene that covered the endpaper. Isaiah 30: 21, New International Version:

Whether you turn to the right or to the left, your ears will hear a voice behind you, saying, "This is the way; walk in it."

Walker looked out at the woods—the real woods—fading in the last of the dusky light. He hadn't heard the voice since the moment his father had come back and knelt in the boy's doorway. He waited, now, but all was quiet. He missed the voice, achingly so at times, but he understood the silence. Sane people didn't hear the Voice of God; that, and Walker didn't really need to hear Him anymore.

The knotty pine door shut quietly, and his father came into the room and rested a hand on his son's shoulder.

Walker closed the scrapbook. The $1 sticker was still on the back. He thought for a moment, then peeled the sticker off and put it in the trash.

His father sat on the mattress and Walker straddled the folding chair, sitting backwards. His father rolled up the cuffs of his workshirt. On his forearm was a raw, pink patch. Walker expected his father to say something about the scar, but he didn't. Instead, he unbuttoned the pocket of his shirt and pulled out a necklace strung with a gold dove ring.

His father held the jewelry out to his son. It sparkled in the amber lamplight. "The FBI found this at the farmhouse," he said.

"After all this time?"

"In fairness, you might say it's a gift to you from the Reverend General."

Walker felt his brow knit.

His father went on, his eyes on the necklace draped across his palm. "He heard how sick you were, what you had seen. His attorney was furious. The necklace is physical evidence linking the Reverend General to your mother's death, but the

Reverend General insisted on telling where it was. He said you should have it, and that he didn't care if the prosecutors added another count for murder. Which they will"—his father looked at him—"if we ask them to. And"—he hesitated—"if you want to testify. Do you want to tell what you heard and saw from the log?"

A long moment passed. "Do we have to decide that now?"

"No. We don't."

Walker stood up from the chair and went over to the dangling necklace. He closed his hand around the dove.

He sighed. Why were all the things the two of them had left of her so cold to the touch? He handed the necklace back to his father, who still wore his own silver dove on his finger. Then he went to the desk and wrote:

Sky, I can't give this to you, but please take care of it for me and one day we will talk about it.

It would be nice to write that he would need the ring back because, someday, he might want to give it to her again, forever. The thought startled him: a light had just flickered across one of the tree trunks in the dark forest. But he didn't write that. Thoughts like that— normal thoughts for a fifteen-year-old boy, he supposed, thoughts about football and school and girlfriends and the future—such thoughts were too much for him right now. So he just signed "Walker."

"Would this be okay with you?" He handed the note to his father.

His father read it, then wrapped the necklace in the paper and gave it back. Walker slipped the note and necklace into his jeans, and his father turned his attention to the packing. As his father began carrying things out of the room, Walker picked up the broom and began to sweep.

He and his father would wait for Sky and Roxanne to close, then the four of them would share a meal in the quiet diner. They would say their goodbyes and, privately, Walker would entrust his mother's wedding ring to his best friend. Father and son would drive up the road one last time, creeping slowly past a dark Airway Deluxe mobile home with the garden gone to weeds, before heading south on 259. Then, with the highway visible only as far as the headlights could illuminate, the two of them would follow the dashed white line.

It wasn't very far ahead to see. Walker tipped the contents of the nearly empty dustpan into the trash and propped the broom. He cranked the window shut, turned off the lamp, and tucked his scrapbook under his arm. But it might be far enough, he thought, as he studied the spare room from the doorway. Headlights could light a very long way, one patch of road at a time.